How to be in a Relationship

KLAUDIA SONAS

Book Cover by Klaudia Sonas

1st edition 2023

To all the single girls in Zurich.
You are worth it.

Prologue

"You're going where?" My mother looked at me as if I had told her I was moving to Mars.

"To Switzerland," I replied for the hundredth time, trying to keep my cool.

"But why would you leave Seattle? You have everything here." She gave me a disapproving look. "What about your job? Your family?"

I sighed. "I'm in love, mum. I can't keep doing the long-distance thing with Tim."

She heard our story many times. It was a warm summer day when fate intervened and Tim, literally, collided with me while out for a jog. In the chaos of the moment, my treasured frappuccino became a casualty, its contents spilling onto the pavement. Apologies turned into conversation, and soon we found ourselves strolling through the picturesque streets, immersed in each other's stories. The connection was instant, the chemistry undeniable. As the sun dipped below the horizon, we shared a spontaneous picnic by the shimmering lake, laughter and affection filling the air. Since then, we've been seeing each other every chance we got.

Mum rolled her eyes dramatically. "Is this still going on with that boy?"

"He's not a boy, mum. He's a grown man," I replied, slightly annoyed.

My mother huffed. "What about settling down and having a family? You're not getting any younger, you know."

I rolled my eyes. "I know, mum. But I'm not settling for just anyone. I've found a man I want to spend the rest of my life with."

My mother still looked unconvinced, but I stood my ground. It was time for me to be closer to my boyfriend. "Why don't we spend these last few days together? Then you can come visit me in Zurich in a few months? You'll see that everything will work out just fine."

My mother sighed, giving in to my persistence. "Fine, but you better not forget about your family. And don't expect me to like fondue."

I chuckled, relieved that she was willing to compromise. "Deal! I'll keep in touch and send you plenty of Swiss chocolate."

She gave me a half-hearted smile. "That's the least you can do."

The plane has finally landed. It took me over fourteen hours to get to Zurich. Connecting flight from Chicago and here I am. To be with my man every day - not just once a month! The air was crisp; the sun was shining. Before landing, I could see the Alps from above. I couldn't wait to get settled.

The wave of nervousness washed over me. I realized I had left my home, my job and my entire life for love. It better be worth it!

As I stepped off the plane, I was greeted by the bustling airport of Zurich. The sounds of people rushing by and the smell of freshly brewed coffee filled the air.

I scanned the crowd, looking for the one person who made this entire journey worth it. And then I saw him.

He was standing near the exit, his eyes locked on me. He was tall, with a charming smile and piercing blue eyes. As I approached him, I could feel my heart beating faster.

"Welcome to Zurich, my love," Tim said, taking my hand and pulling me into a warm embrace.

I melted into his arms, breathing in his scent, the weight of my decision lifting off my shoulders.

Let the adventure begin!

Chapter 1

"Erica! Your phone is buzzing!" Tim bellowed from the bathroom, his voice bouncing off the tiled walls.

An alarm blared in the pitch-black room, rudely interrupting my peaceful slumber. I fumbled around for my phone on the mattress, cursing the wretched noise that penetrated my eardrums.

"What time is it?" I muttered under my breath.

"You're going to be late," he warned me as he appeared in the bedroom doorway, a towel slung around his hips. Sweat glistened across his taut muscles. He had already been for a jog this morning while I was still blissfully asleep. I never work out in the morning. I might later at the gym. No promises, though.

"Coffee?" he asked, leaving the bedroom. He was always full of energy this early in the day!

“Yes, please,” I yawned half-heartedly and stretched like a cat on a couch. The thought of dragging myself to work made me shudder with dread.

It’s been six months since I arrived in Switzerland and boy, has it been a rollercoaster of emotions! Adapting to a new language and culture was no easy feat, but I managed to land a job quickly, which is practically unheard of in Zurich! However, the work is tough and the pressure to meet tight deadlines was constant. Our project’s success could mean everything for the company, so the stakes were high.

When I moved in with Tim, it was a challenge to make his bachelor apartment work for two people. Finding a place to live in this city was no joke. Queues for viewings were miles long and most of the nicer apartments were going to families instead of unmarried couples like us. I could already hear my mother saying it’s a sign for us to get on with making babies! But, despite the challenges, moving to Switzerland had been an exciting adventure for me. Sure, I feel homesick and out of place sometimes, but I was grateful for this opportunity to grow and learn more about myself. Who knows, I might even discover a new side of me I never knew existed! So, I’m taking it one day at a time, embracing the journey, and keeping an open mind.

“Schatz, you better shape up your morning routine or you won’t get anywhere,” he scowled and handed me some coffee. Rich dark espresso with just a whisper of bitterness.

"Aren't you the perfect example of Swiss punctuality?" I grimaced. "I swear, it's like it runs through your veins."

Tim chuckled and planted a kiss on my forehead before jetting out the door. It was amazing how quickly he could throw on his clothes and be ready to go.

"Off you go so I can enjoy these few moments of peace," I muttered under my breath. He was wonderful, but I needed some time to myself.

Being single was my status in the States. At thirty-four, I had a few half-hearted attempts at romance. The business types, the fitness freaks, the sweethearts and the assholes - you name it, I've dated them! But none of them managed to capture my heart for more than a few fleeting dates. No one was the one that made me feel like forever was possible.

My mum had her hopes up, every time to be disappointed that I will not bring a future husband home to meet the family. Until my trip to Zurich, where I clearly fell head over heels for Tim. He was everything I wanted. Well, almost everything, but the distance relationship survived, and it was a clear sign I should drop everything and moving across the globe.

As I sipped on my coffee, my thoughts drifted to the night before. Tim had taken me to a cozy little restaurant in the heart of Zurich. The food was delicious and the wine, even better. We talked for hours, about everything from our families to our dreams and aspirations. It felt like we had known each other for years.

I couldn't believe that I was living with a man! But the reality of leaving everything behind to be with him hit me hard. I had a good job, a significant group of friends, and a comfortable life in the States. Moving to a foreign country where I didn't speak the language, didn't know anyone other than Tim, and had to start from scratch was a daunting thought.

I glanced around the bedroom searching for my slippers, which I had the inexplicable habit of leaving all over the apartment—except for next to the bed. The Swiss floors were cold, no carpets here; a luxury I took for granted back in the States.

Finding my slippers -in the kitchen of all places - I made my way to the bathroom. I was running late, yet my hair needed proper care. It would have to be a quick shower, though. I turned on my favorite Latin-American music and climbed into the shower, immediately picking up speed from its rhythmic beats. Soap, conditioner, face wash, body wash; I attended to all visible areas with a razor and was out in less than ten minutes. A personal record! Looks like that cup of coffee finally did its job.

As I stepped out of the shower, I wrapped a towel around my body and grabbed the hair dryer. Just as I began drying my hair, I heard a doorbell.

I wrapped the towel tighter around my body and made my way to the front door. I hesitated before peeking through the peephole, but curiosity got the best of me.

Through the peephole, I saw a tall, dark-haired Hispanic man standing outside my door. I didn't recognize him, but he had a charming smile and a confident aura around him.

"Can I help you?" I asked, cracking the door.

"Hi, I'm your neighbor," he said, replying in English with a heavy accent. "I live down the hall. I'm sorry to bother you, but I accidentally locked myself out of my apartment and was wondering if I could borrow your phone to call the locksmith."

My gaze lingered on him for a beat longer than I'd intended, suddenly aware that he was waiting for my response.

"Oh- of course!" I exclaimed, the words tumbling out of my mouth.

Frantically trying to hold my towel around my body, I made an attempt at getting my phone that was charging next to the bed.

He patiently waited outside the apartment door for me. In a hurry, I rushed into the bathroom, hastily replacing the towel with a pink and fluffy bathrobe that made me feel more secure in its layers.

Returning to my neighbor, I handed my cell phone and watched as he stood in the stairwell talking to someone in German. I couldn't help but admire his physique as he leaned against the railing. His tight shirt showcased his muscular chest and arms, making me feel a little weak in the knees. As he finished up the phone call, he turned towards me and flashed me the captivating smile.

"Thank you so much for letting me use your phone. I really appreciate it," he said as he handed it back to me.

"No problem at all. I hope everything gets sorted out with your apartment," I replied, trying to sound nonchalant.

He smiled, waved goodbye, and disappeared downstairs.

My heart leaped as the phone buzzed in my hand. Tim's name lit up the screen. "Have you made it to the office yet, Schatz?"

The constant need he had to monitor me was becoming slightly tiresome.

"Em... no, not yet. They canceled the first meeting, so I thought I'd take some time," I lied, though I wasn't sure why I didn't feel like I could tell him the truth. What was wrong with me? But what could I tell him? That some handsome stranger had appeared at our doorstep or, even more, embarrassing that I was taking my sweet time in the morning?

Chapter 2

As soon as I entered the office lobby, I spotted my new best friend, Natalia. We had only just met when I joined the company, but it felt like we'd known each other all our lives. I still kept in touch with my friends back in America, but the time difference made it difficult and our lives were so drastically different now. With every call and conversation, it felt like we drifted farther and farther apart.

Natalia became my closest friend in Zurich and it felt amazing to have someone to talk to about the latest office gossip over a cup of coffee. Her amazing fashion sense made me envious in the early days. She always dressed to impress, wearing feminine and colorful outfits that fit the occasion. And her shoes! Never any flats; she must have had Slavic genes allowing her to carry herself with such grace and poise on those heels.

As I approached her, she turned around and gave me a dazzling smile, revealing her perfect white teeth.

"Hey, girl!" she exclaimed, her accent adding a touch of exoticism to her words. "I've been waiting for you - having late morning?"

I knew she didn't judge. She wasn't an early bird herself and was more often than me arriving late. Natalia worked as a Personal Assistant to Head of Sales - an older gay gentleman who was an angel to work for.

Having little time to chat, seeing as another meeting was coming up, we exchanged a quick kiss on the cheek and promised to meet for lunch. My desk was on a different floor than hers, so I rushed off quickly to make it on time.

A group of people greeted me as I walked into the conference room. They were all discussing the latest project. I took my seat at the head of the table and began the meeting. As a project manager, I had to keep things running smoothly and efficiently, making sure everyone knew their roles and responsibilities. It was a stressful time, so we dived right in. I managed to occupy my mind enough to forget for a moment the eventful morning I had.

Lunch came like a sweet escape, offering a temporary respite from the frustrations of the workday. The executive board wasn't happy with the solution we proposed. One of them even called it *crap* to my face. I made my way to the bustling cafeteria, where Natalia waited for me, having secured a prime spot overlooking the lake. Location of the office was amazing, close to the park and bustling life of Zurich center.

"You look like you need a drink instead of a lunch break," Natalia looked at me, worried.

I let out a heavy sigh and vented, "That project is driving me insane. Nothing we do seems to be right, yet they themselves have no clue what the perfect solution should be."

"Have you tried to talk to your manager?" she asked, throwing her blazer on the chair to mark it taken.

We made our way toward the buffet, the rhythmic clack of Natalia's heels echoing through the cafeteria.

"There's no point. He's even more stressed than I am. Besides, I feel like they just don't want to listen to a woman, let alone an American." Natalia was one of the few people with whom I could be brutally honest. Knowing she understood the complexities of navigating the business world as a foreigner herself. At times, I wondered why feminists fought so ardently for women's rights, yet I cherished the freedom to have a career. However, on days like this, I couldn't help but ponder why bother.

Interrupting my thoughts, Natalia announced. "Well, let's shift our focus from the annoying to the exciting. I have some news."

"Oh?" I raised an eyebrow, anticipating another tale of romance.

"I signed up for salsa classes," she declared, catching me completely off guard.

My laughter escaped before I could stop it. "Dance lessons? Really?" Natalia, the woman who preferred lounging at the bar while guys vied for her attention, was now aspiring to shine on the dance floor?

Unfazed, Natalia nodded and explained, "Everyone learns salsa. It's an essential skill. When your dream man approaches you at a club, you'll be able to dance with him effortlessly."

I looked at her, astounded. This was a side of Natalia I had never witnessed before. She was determined. She pulled out her phone, revealing a video from a lavish party in one of Zurich's poshest clubs. "Look at how they dance! These men are irresistible!"

The bond between Natalia and me wasn't forged by our fashion sense. It was by our shared experience of being single for an extended period. Although I now had Tim in my life, someone I was deeply in love with, I confided in Natalia about my past dating escapades in the States. She, too, revealed that her romantic journey mirrored mine. We were both searching for something, though unsure of what exactly. While Natalia dreamed of a billionaire who was handsome, caring, and romantic, I had more realistic expectations. I knew I'd be content with a millionaire.

Jokes aside, even in my current relationship, I sometimes wondered if Tim was truly happy and if we were destined for a lifelong commitment.

"So anyway, the classes start this Friday," Natalia announced, a suggestive smile playing on her lips.

"Well, you go, girl, and salsa your way through this town!" I chuckled.

"The thing is, Erica," Natalia began, "It's not just me going to the classes. I signed you up as well."

My eyes widened in horror. "No!"

There was simply no way that I, Erica Davis, proud Washingtonian, would subject myself to salsa dancing. Back home, we hiked, drank, and found joy in countless other ways. Dancing had never been part of the equation. My lack of coordination resembled that of someone with two left feet. That's why spending time with Natalia was effortless—we would sit, drink, sing our hearts out, and revel in each other's company.

"You didn't!" I stared at her, panic creeping into my voice.

"I sure did! And I'm certain Tim will appreciate it!" Natalia grinned mischievously.

"Tim hates dancing more than anything! He has always been content leaning against the walls!" I protested.

"Please, do this with me!" Natalia pleaded, her eyes resembling those of a puppy. "It's just six lessons. They speak English, and if you hate it, you can stop."

If anyone else had made this request, I would have continued saying no. But it was Natalia—the woman who had injected a dose of friendship into my otherwise lonely life in Switzerland. I would do this for her. I would dance salsa, even if it meant performing in front of other people.

"Fine," I sighed, surrendering to her plea.

"You won't regret it!" Natalia shrieked with excitement.

Won't I? I asked myself.

Chapter 3

Friday was rapidly approaching, and normally, I would embrace the start of the weekend with open arms. However, this time, the thought of exposing myself in front of others made me feel nauseous. Stepping outside my comfort zone was never my strong suit. I preferred the familiar. I occasionally entertained the idea of trying something new and signed up for it. When the moment arrived, I would often contemplate canceling.

"You literally moved across the ocean for a man! How is this not stepping out of your comfort zone?" Natalia shook her head, refusing to let me back out at the last minute.

"But it was different! I already knew Tim, we had been meeting. This whole thing didn't happen overnight!" I pleaded, attempting to justify my apprehension.

Natalia rolled her eyes. "Jeez, Erica. You act as if I'm taking you to a cult ritual tonight."

"It might as well be," I mumbled under my breath.

"Trying new things won't kill you," Natalia declared before strutting away in her glossy black Louboutins. "See you in two hours in the lobby."

Feeling dissatisfied with my failed mission to cancel, I watched Natalia disappear around the corner. I couldn't help but wonder why she had become so insistent about this dancing endeavor. And those new Louboutins—where did she get them? They must have cost a fortune! Had she made a deal with the fashion devil, or could she actually afford them on her personal assistant pension?

Two hours later, as unfortunately promised, I waited in the lobby for Natalia. I was wondering what one brings to the dance class. I haven't thought of a change of clothes as I decided the office ones would do. I was wearing a black sleeveless top and black chinos paired with a pair of beige ballerinas. I decided it must be enough for the first lesson and I wouldn't be standing out of the crowd too much.

Natalia met me downstairs. She changed into a red carmen dress flowing around her knees. She was still wearing her mesmerizing shoes.

"Aren't you changing?" she looked at me suspiciously. "You're still coming, right?"

I nodded. 'I will check it all out first before I take out my dance costume.'

Natalia snorted. "Fine. Thank you for doing this for me." She hugged me and I felt better about the whole thing. I was doing it for my best friend. It's fine. The sacrifices we do for a friendship are the karmic points we can use later in life.

"So where is the school?" I asked, following Natalia to her car. I was used to taking the public transport. Tim insisted on it. He believed there was no need for a car in the city, and with Switzerland's efficient transportation system, he had a point. Natalia coming from Eastern Europe couldn't fathom going anywhere without a car, taxi, or Uber.

"We're going to park near the bridge downtown and from there it's just two blocks away."

We rolled out in her sky blue BMW and joined the other commuters in the long line of traffic. Friday evenings were absolutely terrible for traveling by car. The streets were congested and we had to wait ten minutes on every crossing. After what felt like an eternity, we finally reached our destination.

I stepped out of Natalia's car and stretched my body, feeling the stiffness from sitting for too long. We walked the two blocks until we arrived at a tall building. I tried to relax and reassure myself that everything would be fine. No one was going to make fun of me; after all, we were all beginners. I repeated that thought like a mantra until we reached the door of the dance school on the second floor. In bold red letters on a yellow background, it proudly displayed the name SALSA PARAISO, accompanied by a silhouette of a woman in a dancing pose.

"Ready?" Natalia turned to me and winked.

"Definitely," I replied, but under my breath, I added, "Not." Relax, Erica. It will be fine.

Natalia had made all the arrangements in advance, so we simply walked to the end of the corridor and joined the others, waiting for the previous lesson to finish. To my relief, everyone seemed equally petrified. The men, in particular, appeared as if they might bolt at any moment.

"Okay, maybe it won't be as bad as I thought," I muttered to myself.

Natalia, standing beside me, started giggling uncontrollably. "No way!" she exclaimed. "What a coincidence!"

I turned to see what had caught her attention and spotted a tall, handsome man approaching. He wasn't my type, a bit too mature for my taste, but he seemed to have made an impression on Natalia.

"Natalia? What a pleasant surprise to see you here!" The man took her hand in both of his. "I had no idea you were learning salsa too?"

I watched their interaction, trying to comprehend what was happening. Suddenly, it dawned on me.

Clearing my throat, I turned to Natalia. "Natalia, um, do you have a moment?" My gaze urged her to follow me.

"What's up?" she asked innocently.

"Is this the reason we're at this ridiculous dance school?" I seethed. "Because you wanted to 'coincidentally' meet this guy?"

Natalia looked down, sheepish. "Well, I didn't tell you the whole truth," she admitted. "I knew if I told you, you'd never come with me."

"Unbelievable! It was all for a guy! I knew it!"

"Come on, please. I really like him, and what better way to get to know someone than through dancing?" She pleaded, flashing those puppy eyes.

"I've never heard you say anything like that before!"

"Well, I mean, Roman might have said it..."

"Is Roman the guy staring at you right now with a look like he's won the lottery?" I interrupted. Indeed, the man named Roman appeared thrilled to have Natalia in his salsa class.

Before I could scold her any further, the door to the dance studio swung open, and people streamed out. A petite woman stuck her head out and called, "Salsa beginners, come on in!"

"Yes, announce to the entire world that we don't know how to dance," I sighed.

Natalia walked over to Roman and introduced me as her *bestest friend in the world*. Nice try, I thought. I mouthed to her, "I still haven't forgiven you." She winked in response and joined the others inside the studio.

As the remaining attendees left their belongings on the bench against the wall and changed their shoes. Natalia pulled out her proper dancing shoes and left her Louboutins on the side. That girl was determined!

"Alright, everyone!" the petite woman clapped her hands. "Nico will join us in a moment, and until then, let's do a warm-up."

She guided us through shoulder circles and neck stretches, and my body was more at ease. This was a good start—I could handle it. It would be fine.

Just as we were getting into the rhythm of the warm-up, the door swung open, and all eyes turned to the man entering the room.

I froze.

Oh no, this can't be happening! The last time this man saw me, I was wearing nothing but a towel around my naked body, with no makeup and hair that resembled an electrocution aftermath!

Chapter 4

Nico, the salsa teacher, turned out to be my neighbor as well! I must have looked bewildered because Natalia nudged me, her curiosity evident. "What's going on?" she whispered, noticing my gaze fixed on Nico, who now stood at the front of the class. I discreetly took a few steps back to ensure everyone else was in front of me.

Earlier this week, I had told Natalia about the unexpected encounter I had with Nico at my doorstep. She found it amusing, but had thought little of it. "Honey," she had said dismissively, "if I made a big deal out of every guy who knocks on my door, I'd lose my mind." Now, she was perplexed why it seemed to be affecting me so much.

"It's my neighbor," I whispered to Natalia. Her eyes widened with understanding. "Oh, the one who showed up at your door! I didn't realize he was so young!" she added, struggling to suppress her laughter.

The music ended, and Nico, along with his co-teacher, Isabelle, smiled at the group. Peering over Roman's shoulder, I caught a glimpse of Nico's dazzling smile. He was tall and had an effortless charm about him. His broad shoulders looked striking in a simple black T-shirt paired with black jeans and white trainers.

"Hello, everyone!" Isabelle greeted. "Welcome to Salsa Paraiso! We're thrilled that you've joined us, and we can't wait to embark on this salsa adventure together!"

Nico grabbed a notepad and pen from the nearby desk. "Let's check the attendance list, shall we?"

A shiver ran down my spine. He's going to recognize me. Nico began calling out the names, and with each person, he looked closely, trying to match faces to names. He greeted everyone warmly, smiling at their responses.

"Erica?" Nico called out, scanning the room for a raised hand.

"She's here," I heard Natalia speaking. It seemed good enough for Nico. He continued down the list until the final name, Robert, was called.

Lucky break. Keep flying under the radar, and he'll never discover who you are.

Clapping his hands, Nico exclaimed, "Wonderful! We have an equal number of ladies and gentlemen, which will come in handy later when we dance in pairs. For now, let's learn some basic merengue steps. We'll delve into salsa later tonight."

I exhaled in relief. He hadn't recognized me. At least for the next hour or so, we wouldn't be doing couple dancing, giving me some time to process everything. The guilt washed over me as I thought about Tim, completely unaware of the situation unfolding here. I hadn't been fully present, reacting on autopilot. After all, I loved my boyfriend, and I had come to Switzerland for him. It was just a silly encounter where a handsome guy caught me at my worst. That was the crux of it—I was such a perfectionist, wanting no one from the outside to witness me in such a state.

But now I looked presentable. Besides, he might not even recognize me, considering I had looked like a sleep-deprived zombie before the caffeine kicked in properly.

We began practicing the merengue steps. Without music playing, I focused on the movement of my feet.

Isabelle clapped. They sure did like clapping here.

"Great! Wonderful! Let's do this one last time, and then we'll try some steps as couples."

Looking around, I searched for a potential partner. The closest person to me was a thin guy with thick glasses and a flannel shirt. I smiled at him, trying to encourage him to pair up, but he averted his gaze quickly, as if he might faint. Well, that was a successful attempt.

When the music stopped, Nico instructed the men to find a partner. The nerdy guy almost sprinted away from me, heading toward a short girl on the other side. Just my luck. However, an older gentleman appeared next to me, asking for my hand. “Shall we, darling?” he smiled, reminiscent of my father. I smiled back, feeling comfortable right away. Natalia, of course, was already standing next to Roman. I’d definitely be calling in a favor from her in the future—a big one!

“Let’s try the merengue together! Remember, ladies, the man leads, not the other way around!” Isabelle reminded us.

Nico started the music, and we began counting the beats. I did my best to follow along, relieved that the merengue was easy enough. My partner seemed to know what he was doing as well, and I hoped we didn’t look too bad. I discreetly glanced in Nico’s direction, ensuring he wasn’t watching me closely.

“Change partners!” Nico’s voice cut through the music. I looked at my current partner, confusion evident on my face. What was happening?

“You go to the next one,” he explained. “We’re rotating.”

I looked to the side for the nerdy guy standing alone, waiting for me. Beads of sweat formed on his forehead, and I hurried over to him.

“One, two, one, two!” Isabelle’s voice counted out the rhythm, guiding our movements.

The nerdy guy and I were trying our best. Before it could get too disastrous, Nico called for us to change partners again. And again. And again. Surprisingly, I was getting the hang of it. I had relaxed to the point where I didn't realize what was about to happen when Nico uttered those words once more: "Change partners!"

I turned around, expecting to find another student, but instead, I found myself face to face with Nico. He extended his arms, waiting for me to join him on the dance floor. Isabelle was already dancing with a student behind him. There was no escape. I took a deep breath and told myself to just go for it, even if my internal pep talk had never worked in moments like this.

"Erica, right?" Nico smiled, displaying the most dazzling smile I had ever seen. Natalia was right, he looked very young. Something I hadn't noticed when he surprised me at my door. I had been too preoccupied with my zombie-like appearance.

With trembling steps, I approached him, and our hands met. The moment our skin touched, a powerful jolt ran through my entire body. What on earth was happening?

"Oh, oops! Sorry," he laughed. "I think it's called static discharge in English?"

Right. I felt utterly foolish. I had mistaken a ridiculous event for some inexplicable connection. It was just a strange occurrence that could happen to anyone.

Nico took hold of my arm, positioned it on his broad shoulder, and grabbed my other hand. He led me through the steps, his closeness suffocating me. He continued smiling, counting the beats to make it easier, and I tried my best not to focus on my feet the entire time. Static discharge or not, I couldn't help but feel a growing concern.

We changed partners a few more times throughout the lesson. The rest of the time, everyone practiced individually, following Nico and Isabelle's steps. Through the glass door, I could see another group of students eagerly waiting for their lesson.

"Thank you, everyone!" Isabelle clapped, signaling the end of the lesson.

"See you next week! Great progress!" Nico beamed. Not once did he give me an indication that he recognized me tonight.

I glanced at Natalia, but she was engrossed in flirting with Roman. The hope of grabbing a drink together after class quickly faded. A walk home seemed like a better idea to clear my mind. Fortunately, Nico was teaching another class after mine, so I wouldn't have to stress about running into him on the staircase.

As darkness settled, I strolled along, enjoying the sight of the lake. Switzerland was a stark contrast to America. Here, a woman could walk at night without feeling in danger. Summer in the city was truly wonderful, and Zurich's cleanliness and lush greenery never ceased to amaze me. I often wondered how they kept it so tidy, until one night, I spotted the cleaning crews bustling about when everyone else was asleep.

Finally, I reached my building and looked up. Our flat was on the second floor, but which one was Nico's? I was only curious, so I could avoid that floor at all costs. The light in our window was on, indicating Tim was home. Lately, he had been working long hours, navigating the turbulent times of his tech startup's first year hoping to secure future success.

"I'm back!" I called out, leaving my bag in the hall.

"In here!" Tim's voice echoed from the living room. I found him on the sofa, his attention glued to his phone as he furiously typed away.

"So done with salsa for good?" he remarked without looking up, his tone laced with indifference.

I was taken aback by his comment. Did he know about Nico? Why would he say that?

"What do you mean?" I asked, trying to mask my unease.

"Well, it must have been an awful experience, no? And let's face it, you're not exactly a skilled dancer," he smirked, finally glancing up from his phone.

I couldn't determine if he was joking or being serious. "Well, actually, I might give it another go," I replied, mustering some defiance.

Tim raised an eyebrow, a hint of surprise in his eyes. "Seriously? What happened to my Erica?"

"Your Erica is still here," I retorted, growing annoyed. We often engaged in playful banter, but this felt different.

Tim didn't respond; he simply shrugged, dismissing my words.

"Are you okay?" I asked, studying his expression with a concern.

Just as I spoke, Tim's phone rang, causing him to jolt towards the kitchen. "I have to take this," he muttered, closing the door behind him.

As I sank into the sofa, enveloped in a cozy blanket, I couldn't help but ponder the situation. Was all of this normal? One evening, we shared a romantic dinner, and the next, I received a chilly reception. As a newcomer to relationships, I realized I had no idea how they truly worked, and it left me with a sense of uncertainty.

Chapter 5

Saturday mornings were my favorite time of the week. I would relish the luxury of sleeping in, savoring a cup of coffee, and indulging in a few hours of uninterrupted reading in bed. It was my sanctuary, a time reserved just for me. However, since arriving here, I couldn't shake off the feeling that such leisurely mornings were somehow frowned upon. Tim, an early riser by nature, expected me to align my schedule with his.

It hadn't always been this way. Six months ago, when I first arrived, he would lovingly snuggle up with me, bringing coffee and croissants to bed, eager to share the details of his work. But over time, those cozy mornings together had become increasingly scarce, and I wasn't even sure if I would see him in the morning anymore. Building a business was undoubtedly demanding, but nurturing a relationship required effort as well. Each person had expectations, and if we failed to meet each other halfway, we risked facing disappointment in the long run.

I heard Tim busying himself in the kitchen. Well, at least he was still here. I remembered last night and the strange welcome I received. Sometimes I wondered if it was the vibe I was sending out that influenced others around me. People always seemed to sense when something was amiss. Yesterday, the emotions stirred within me by Nico had left me consumed by an overwhelming sense of guilt. Did Tim pick up on it too? I had done nothing wrong, yet this remorse weighed heavily on me. I found myself entangled in a complicated web, unsure of where I stood or how Tim perceived the situation.

I walked into the kitchen, no slippers in sight, and saw Tim hastily devouring a croissant with a cup of coffee in hand, his gaze fixed on the pages of Neue Zurcher Zeitung. His eyes lifted from the newspaper as he caught sight of me.

"Good morning, sleepyhead," he greeted me with a warm smile. "How are your muscles feeling after yesterday?"

Surprised by his gentle inquiry, I looked at him, and there it was, the Tim I knew and loved. "I wouldn't exactly call our first lesson a strenuous workout," I replied, returning the smile. "But I enjoyed it. It was something different, you know? Yesterday was so stressful at work, and it helped me unwind a little."

Tim continued to gaze at me, his piercing blue eyes conveying a depth of emotion. “How about we snuggle back in bed?” he suggested.

A rush of warmth flooded my chest, and I couldn’t help but feel a surge of happiness. “Yes, please!” I exclaimed, giggling as I hopped back onto the bed, eagerly awaiting Tim’s company. Today was going to be a great day. I just knew it!

As wonderful as cuddles were, Tim disappeared, right after saying he was going for a jog and then straight into the office. I tried to sound understanding, wishing him a productive day, but deep down, I felt disappointed to be abandoned on the weekend. Determined to make the most of my day, I decided to explore Zurich on my own. With Tim, work, and the whirlwind of leaving home behind, I hadn’t had enough time to truly experience the city that was now my home. Swiftly changing into comfortable clothes and slipping on my sneakers, I ventured out the door. As I descended the stairs, I heard footsteps approaching. I turned the corner and found myself face to face with Nico.

My heart skipped a beat. I wasn’t ready to face him just yet, especially after what happened yesterday. In a moment of panic, I contemplated running back to my apartment, but I didn't want to come across as a complete weirdo.

"Erica! Good morning!" his face lit up. "How did you like the class yesterday?"

I blushed. "Hello, Nico." He didn't seem confused about neighbor and salsa student situation. "I enjoyed myself, thank you."

He grinned. "If you ever have questions, I'm just downstairs."

"So you got the door open, then?" I relaxed slightly.

He chuckled. "If not, I'd probably be knocking at your door, asking if there's a couch I could sleep on."

Horror flashed across my eyes. What would Tim think?

"I'm kidding!" he quickly added, placing his hand on my shoulder. And there it was again—the electric current coursing through my entire body. No static discharge this time.

Nico studied my face. "Is everything okay?"

I cleared my throat, mustering composure. "Yes, of course!" My voice pitched a little higher than I would have liked. "Anyway, I'm glad it all worked out."

He continued to gaze at me, and after what felt like an eternity, he finally said, "I'll see you next Friday at salsa, then."

I nodded and hastened downstairs. I wanted to steal a glance to see if he was still there, but I didn't dare. Flushed and perspiring, I practically sprinted out of the building, relishing the embrace of the fresh air. What on earth was happening?

I dialed Natalia's number. It rang ten times before she finally picked up.

"Were you still asleep?" I asked. I didn't really care at this point. I needed her. I was a terrible friend.

Natalia released a tremendous yawn before responding. "I'm awake. What's up?"

"Coffee at Starbucks?" I asked hopefully.

"Girl, when will you realize we have better cafes than that?" Natalia snorted. "I'll meet you at Babu's in an hour." She hung up.

I had an hour to kill, so I decided to browse the local bookshop. English books were pricey and not much to pick from, but I liked taking a stroll among the shelves and watching people.. It was something I could indulge in before Natalia arrived. She could never comprehend my love for reading. Her idea of a great time involved sipping cocktails at the lakeside bar, eyeing attractive men, and indulging in gossip. Not that I had anything against it, but selecting a good book now and then was a pleasure I didn't want to pass up.

I found myself perusing the self-help section when a text from Tim popped up. *I'll be stuck here until late. Will you be okay by yourself?*

It was becoming frustrating. *I had hoped we would spend time together...* I replied.

Erica, I have to work. Why don't you go for a run or have that German class you booked a while back?

Dang. I had completely forgotten about that stupid German class I had signed up for online. Neither jogging nor attending a German class sounded like a fun way to spend my Saturday. Frustrated with Tim, I fired back a text, "Actually, Natalia just called and invited me for a girls' night out."

Tim's reply came almost immediately. "Dancing again? Why not spend your time doing something more productive?" I didn't bother replying. Another text arrived shortly after, "Text me the address of the club."

I sighed. Not only did he not want to spend time with me, but he also felt the need to check up on me from afar. Well, now Natalia and I had to go out. I didn't want to be labeled indecisive. Hopefully, she had the time and no plans with Roman or anyone else.

As I scanned the bookshelves, one cover caught my attention: '*How to Be Single: A Workbook for Embracing New Freedom.*' I rolled my eyes. What I needed was a workbook called 'How to Be in a Relationship.'

Chapter 6

"Of course we're going out!" Natalia squeaked with excitement. "Wonderful idea! Come over to my place before, and we'll have a makeover!"

She was ecstatic, and her enthusiasm was contagious. I couldn't help but smile at her energy. Maybe it was a good idea to go out tonight. Maybe it would be fun, a chance to let loose and gain a fresh perspective on everything that was happening.

"Would it be just us girls?" I cautiously asked, not wanting to be the odd one out if she decided to invite Roman along.

"Sure thing," she replied, but then her gaze dropped, her expression changing.

"Natalia, is everything okay?" I asked, concern filling my voice. One moment she seemed elated, and the next something seemed off. 'Is it Roman?'

She let out a sigh. “Ah, Erica. Sometimes I wonder if I’ll ever find someone. Hearing you talk about Tim’s behavior, I’m starting to question the whole idea of relationships.”

“But I thought you were happy just dating,” I said, genuinely surprised by her sudden desire to settle down.

“I do enjoy dating and the thrill of it all,” she explained. “But at some point, I want more. The problem is, either the guy turns out to be a complete jerk, or we’re just fundamentally different people.”

Her words resonated with me. It was as if she had summed up my entire dating history. That is until I met Tim. Even though we were complete opposites, we didn’t care. Our chemistry was undeniable, and it was all that mattered. But now, that chemistry was facing its own challenges, struggling to keep us happy.

“Anyway,” Natalia cleared her throat, shifting the conversation. “I really like Roman, but I can’t shake this feeling that something could go wrong at any moment.”

“You can’t think that way!” I tried to comfort her, masking the fear that mirrored her own. “Happily ever after is possible!”

“Does it really happen, though?” she asked, her gaze drifting towards the window.

I wondered what my chances would be in the Swiss dating world if Tim and I didn’t work out. The thought sent a shiver down my spine. I didn’t want to start from scratch again. This was just a rough patch. I believed Tim and I would find our way back to each other.

A tiny voice inside me whispered the name Nico, suggesting he could be an option. I shook my head vigorously, as if trying to dispel that thought from my mind. I couldn't let temptation or uncertainty lead me astray. Let's not challenge fate even more, I thought.

Tim hadn't returned home before I left for Natalia's place. I hadn't heard from him since his last text. His demand to know the club's name was strange. I didn't even know where Natalia was taking me. I decided Tim shouldn't expect to keep tabs on me when he himself was out all day. Maybe I was being a bad girlfriend by not being more understanding about his work and commitments. But he had also committed himself to me.

Natalia swung open her door, holding two flutes of prosecco, with loud music pouring out from her apartment.

"How did you manage to open the door?" I chuckled, seeing her struggling to balance the full glasses in her hands.

"You don't want to know," she laughed. "Come on in!"

I thought to myself that this was exactly what I needed—a cocktail, a makeover, and a girls' night out. What could go wrong?

Natalia had truly outdone herself. Clothes, makeup, and shoes filled her small studio apartment. Her wardrobe was a sight to behold, taking up nearly half the space. I wondered what she had in store for me. Glancing at her tiny waist and long legs, I began to doubt if I would even fit into anything, being an average size 10.

"Try this on!" she tossed something sparkly in my direction. Struggling to make sense of the piece of fabric, I noticed my phone lighting up. I ignored it, convinced it was Tim, and I didn't want the fun to be spoiled.

"I can't possibly fit into this!" I shouted to Natalia, who was busy doing her hair in the bathroom.

"Just pick whatever you like then!" she shouted back, spraying copious amounts of hairspray onto her locks.

I began rummaging through her clothes, trying to find something suitable. Although in Zurich, anything was appropriate. Whether you went to a pub in an elegant dress or a club in jeans, people did as they pleased. However, I didn't want to look like a slob next to Natalia, who was clearly bringing her A-game for the evening.

"Where are we going?" I asked, hoping to narrow down my outfit choices.

"Just wear something sexy!" she walked out with immaculate and voluminous hair. She topped off my glass. "We're going to Plaza. It's Glitter Gewitter tonight!"

Glitter storm party. Oh dear, I had heard about those. Buckets of glitter thrown randomly at people—madness. But, of course, why would Natalia settle for anything less? Let the party begin!

"Goodness, what am I going to wear then?" I continued sifting through her wardrobe, feeling indecisive. It seemed to mirror my life—I struggled to make choices. When I didn't have something, I yearned for it, but once I got it, everything seemed to turn sour.

"That's what you're wearing," Natalia declared, producing a sheer black spaghetti strap dress. "Try it on."

The dress fit me perfectly, accentuating my curves in all the right places. It was knee-length and backless. I was genuinely surprised when I caught a glimpse of myself in the mirror. I looked good. Like, really good. How was it possible for a simple piece of clothing to change my entire perspective?

"Amazing!" Natalia exclaimed, appearing by my side, looking stunning herself. She wore a black and gold striped wrap dress with long golden earrings. "Lose the bra, babe."

I stared at her in shock. "What do you mean?"

"You can't wear a backless dress with a bra," Natalia explained matter-of-factly.

I gulped. Sure, I had a nice pair, but could they handle going braless? Would I be able to handle it?

"Don't worry," Natalia reassured me with a mischievous grin. "We'll fix them up."

This girl had the entire arsenal of tricks to make a dress work for you, not against you. I trusted her expertise and took the plunge. After all, it was time to step out of my comfort zone and embrace the sexy side for a change.

The music was blasting; the prosecco was working its magic, and Natalia was meticulously working on my makeup, enhancing my features. Finally, we were ready to go. I looked at myself in the mirror, and I almost couldn't recognize the Erica staring back at me. The transformation was astounding.

"Wow, thanks Natalia!" I exclaimed, genuinely grateful for her efforts.

"My pleasure, darling! I love your cute outfits, but I'm glad you let me turn you into a sexy girl tonight," she replied, her eyes twinkling with excitement.

I adored Natalia for many reasons, but her unwavering support and non-judgmental nature made our friendship special. In a world where pretty girls often seemed judgmental and patronizing, she was a breath of fresh air.

We finished the rest of the prosecco, feeling the anticipation building up within us, and made our way outside. Natalia checked her phone briefly, her expression shifting, but she quickly composed herself. She hailed an Uber, and we stood on the bustling street of Zurich, waiting for our ride.

The car arrived, and a driver named Todor jumped out to open the door for us. It was clear Natalia captivated him as he enthusiastically entertained us during the entire journey. Finally, we arrived in front of the club. The driver, in a desperate attempt, asked Natalia out on a date. She giggled and gracefully dismissed him. She was used to men behaving like this.

As we said our goodbyes, I realized I had left my phone back at Natalia's place. "Damn," I muttered under my breath, hoping that Tim wouldn't freak out.

But before I could dwell on it, Natalia grabbed my hand, her eyes gleaming with excitement.

"Ready to dance the worries away?" she asked, giving the bouncer a dazzling smile that made him wave us through, bypassing the long queue.

With a deep breath, I stepped into the vibrant world of the Plaza, feeling both nervous and excited. I was ready to let go of my inhibitions and embrace the night ahead. Hopefully, it would provide the distraction and inner clarity I desperately sought.

Chapter 7

The dancefloor pulsed with energy as I stepped onto it, the thumping bass reverberating through my body. The atmosphere was electric, filled with a dazzling array of lights and the promise of a wild night ahead. Just as I was about to make my way to the bar, Natalia tugged me in a different direction, her eyes gleaming with excitement.

"We're heading to the VIP section!" she shouted over the music.

My eyebrows shot up in surprise. VIP section? How on earth did Natalia secure access to this exclusive area? The club was divided into two parts, one for the regular crowd and the other reserved for the privileged few. I always wondered who Natalia knew, but I never imagined she had the connections to enter the elite area.

The pulsating beat of the music filled the VIP section as Natalia and I entered the exclusive area. I couldn't help but be in awe of the luxury surrounding us. Mirrors lined the walls, reflecting the lights, and velvet sofas provided seating for the elegant guests. Men in crisp white suits wearing expensive watches mingled with women. Ladies were wearing gorgeous, body-hugging dresses and towering stilettos. The air was infused with the scent of fine perfumes, and clinking champagne glasses filled the room as people celebrated.

"How did you manage this?" I shouted over the music, unable to contain my curiosity.

Natalia giggled, her voice barely audible above the music. "I have my contacts!"

It must have been one of her posh dates. I was worried that they had made a deal, and now I would be caught in an uncomfortable situation, feeling like a third wheel..

My suspicions proved true. An impeccably dressed older gentleman made his way towards us, exuding an air of sophistication that surpassed anyone else in the room. As a beam of light illuminated his face, my breath caught in my throat. He was old. Like way too old for Natalia! She opened her arms and rushed into a warm embrace with him.

"Uncle!" she cried.

Wait, what? Uncle? As in Natalia's uncle? I did not expect that!

"This is Erica!" Natalia introduced me and I shook the man's hand.

"Welcome, my dear," he greeted me with a heavy Eastern European accent. "I hope you'll enjoy yourselves! Champagne on me!" he offered with a warm smile.

"Thank you!" I replied, gratitude washing over me. What an incredible treat this was turning out to be.

Natalia exchanged a few more sentences with her uncle and waved goodbye.

"I had no idea you had a fancy uncle!" I exclaimed.

Natalia motioned for us to take a seat on a corner sofa, marked with a reserved label. She moved it aside and settled down. "My uncle owns Plaza," she revealed.

I was awestruck. "Wow! I didn't know!" I admitted, surprised that she had never mentioned it before. "So, does your family live here as well?"

Natalia's gaze dropped. "No, they're back home. They never understood how my uncle could leave and settle here. And when I followed, I became disappointment number two," she shrugged, her voice filled with a mix of resignation and strength. "They are quite conservative, and they don't approve of a lifestyle like this."

My eyes scanned the extravagance that surrounded us, and a realization struck me: I had underestimated Natalia. We hadn't talked enough about our families or our struggles in life much since we'd met. But at that moment, I understood how strong she was to break away from her family's expectations and become the incredible person she was today.

Just as the beats of the music pulsed through the air, a waiter materialized before us, holding a gleaming bottle of Moët and two delicate crystal flutes. Our earlier prosecco had long disappeared from our systems, and it was time to replenish the bubbles and fully embrace the night ahead.

From our vantage point in the VIP section, the dance floor below appeared smaller, a sea of moving bodies illuminated by swirling lights. I leaned out from the balcony, taking in the electrifying scene. Some guests from the exclusive area made their way downstairs, merging with the lively crowd. The others remained in the elevated sanctuary, savoring their privileged position. As someone who had only recently embraced the joy of dancing, I was content to stay upstairs. The pulsating rhythms filled the air, infusing the atmosphere with an intoxicating energy. Natalia took out her phone, and we took some selfies. Laughter bubbled between us as we struck playful poses. The evening was really fun!

Just as we settled back into the plush surroundings, Natalia's phone illuminated with an incoming message. She glanced at the screen, a flicker of annoyance crossing her face before she swiftly tucked the device away.

"Everything okay?" I inquired, noticing the subtle shift in her mood.

Natalia flashed a reassuring smile, dismissing any concerns. "Sure!" she replied, effortlessly masking her earlier annoyance.

"Hello Ladies!" someone approached us. With a charming lean, he whispered something into Natalia's ear, eliciting a genuine chuckle from her. Taking this as an invitation, he smoothly settled into the seat beside her, seamlessly integrating himself into our circle. I was hardly surprised. This happened everywhere we went. She possessed a magnetic allure that effortlessly attracted attention from the opposite sex. Sometimes it made me feel insecure, but today I felt amazing in my elegant dress, sitting in a fancy place and sipping on an amazing champagne. What more could a girl ask for?

As if a fate decided to play a prank on me, my gaze shifted towards the far corner of the room, where the crowd seemed to thin out. And there, surrounded by fancy people, stood the man who had occupied my thoughts more than I cared to admit. What on earth was he doing here?

Nico appeared to be in his element. He was wearing a sharp white suit that really brought out his complexion. Talking and joking around with the others, he seemed so different from the man I had seen before. He had cast off his shyness and was now radiating poise and assurance.

My heart suddenly leaped inside my chest when a beautiful woman standing next to him whisked his shoulder. It stirred unexpected feelings of envy within me. In that moment, the memory of Tim, absent from this grand affair, surged back, leaving a twinge of unease in the pit of my stomach. I silently hoped that Tim wouldn't cause a fuss when he realized I had left my phone behind at Natalia's place.

"Isn't this Nico?" Natalia's voice jolted me from my thoughts, causing me to jump slightly. The man who had been vying for her attention had vanished, leaving her fully engaged in our conversation once again. "What is he doing here?"

I shrugged, my confusion mirroring Natalia's. Clearly, Nico's life held more excitement than I had ever imagined. "Didn't you say he was your neighbor?" Natalia questioned, her voice tinged with genuine bewilderment.

I nodded, grappling with the same question. Why wasn't Nico living in a lavish lakeside villa, like the elite gathering around us suggested? Was there something else going on behind the scenes that I didn't know about?

Chapter 8

I tried my best to enjoy the rest of the night, resisting the temptation to glance over at Nico and his lively group of friends who were celebrating in the corner. Various guys, each competing for our attention, constantly approached us. With Tim so busy these days, the simplest compliments got lost under the layers of routine.

The champagne was helping to let go and have fun. As the night progressed, nature called, and I excused myself from Natalia and the others, making my way towards the restroom.

In the ladies' room, the air was filled with the voices of young women putting on makeup. They chattered away excitedly about extravagant boat trips and the guys they were interested in. They discussed how it seemed impossible to remain young and desirable without spending countless hours at beauty salons. Listening to them speak so readily about all these pressures made me feel heavy-hearted; this world that they lived in was one I still had yet to fully comprehend.

I fixed my makeup, added an extra layer of a red lipstick and fluffed my chestnut hair. This should do. I left the bathroom and walked towards our corner. But before I could reach it, a warm, gentle hand gripped my arm, sending an electric shiver down my spine. I knew, without even looking, who that was.

"Nico!" I smiled, trying not to sound too eager.

"Erica!" he exclaimed. "Running into you so often lately!"

"Do you come here often?" I asked.

"Just a night out with friends!" he replied.

I nodded, my heart racing, desperate to tell him how his touch sent me into a dizzying whirlwind, how his smile had the power to hypnotize me. But I kept it to myself, limiting our conversation to the usual pleasantries.

His gaze locked with mine, his chocolate eyes filled with an intensity that threatened to unravel me completely. If not for the physical restraint of my body, I feared I would melt right there on the dance floor.

Natalia hurried over to us, interrupting the moment that was unfolding. "Erica! We have to go!" she exclaimed, her urgency cutting through the air.

My heart sank. Natalia's expression seemed serious, and I could tell she wasn't joking. Nico glanced between Natalia and me, confused, trying to make sense of the situation.

Natalia pulled me away, whispering in my ear, "Tim is here!"

Tim? How did he know where we were? What was he doing here at this hour? Panic coursed through my veins, turning the vibrant atmosphere into a nightmare.

"I'm so sorry, Nico, but we have an emergency," I apologized, my words rushed. Without waiting for his response, we made our way towards the exit of the VIP section. Descending the stairs, I spotted Tim's silhouette, his arms crossed and a deep frown etched on his face.

"Tim! What are you doing here?" I blurted out, my voice revealing my surprise and the alcohol that lingered in my system.

"They wouldn't let me in!" Tim scoffed, his gaze shifting towards the bouncer. "I've been trying to reach you! You never replied!"

I didn't want to cause a scene in Natalia's uncle's club. I rushed outside, Natalia a few steps behind us, giving us some privacy.

"I forgot my phone at Natalia's," I sighed, attempting to diffuse the tension. "I'm fine, Tim."

"How was I supposed to know? You never told me where you were going!" Tim's frustration grew by the minute.

Natalia kept glancing at us, making sure I was okay. "How did you know I was here, then?" I demanded.

"I texted Natalia," he motioned towards my best friend. "She also took her sweet time replying!"

"You keep her out of this, Tim," I gritted my teeth. He will not blame Natalia for his recent need to control me! "I went out to have a good time since you decided work was more important."

"I'm sorry I'm trying to make something out of myself!" he was offended. "I didn't go out drinking like you!" He looked at me top to bottom, shaking his head. "What are you even wearing?!"

The fight was getting very heated. Natalia took a few steps towards us, concerned, but I gestured for her to stay back. I needed to deal with Tim alone.

My voice remained steady, despite the champagne-induced haze. "I am going to say goodbye to my friend, and then you're going to order us a taxi." With that, I walked away towards Natalia, leaving Tim to cool down.

Horror filled Natalia's eyes as she apologized, "I'm so sorry! He kept texting me, so I finally gave him the address. I didn't think he'd actually show up here."

I embraced her, assuring her, "Don't blame yourself. You did nothing wrong. Tim is just overreacting."

"I didn't expect Nico to be there either; otherwise, I wouldn't have replied to Tim's texts," Natalia whispered, her voice filled with regret.

"Everything will be fine. Tim doesn't have a clue," I reassured her. Despite my fleeting attraction to Nico, there was nothing going on between us, merely innocent conversations. Tim's possessiveness and lack of attention left me yearning for more, but I remained faithful.

"The taxi is here!" Tim's voice snapped me back to reality.

I squeezed Natalia goodbye and ran towards the taxi. The ride home was suffocatingly silent, and soon we were climbing the stairs to our apartment. Rather than continuing the argument, I headed straight for the bathroom, locking the door behind me. I hoped Tim wouldn't follow, needing some time to wash off the glitter, stress, and alcohol while attempting to clear my head.

Emerging from the bathroom, I felt the tension hanging in the air. Our small apartment suddenly felt even smaller. Bracing myself for round two of the argument, I walked into the living room only. Tim sat on the sofa with his laptop open and his phone next to him, engrossed in work. At two in the morning! I couldn't believe it. Here he was, acting as if nothing had happened, as if he hadn't caused a scene at the club. As if he hadn't said hurtful things to me. Anger welled up inside me, but I swallowed it down, determined not to let it consume me.

"Are you going to bed?" I asked, my voice laced with a mix of frustration and exhaustion.

Tim shook his head without even looking up from his laptop. "I need to finish this," he replied curtly.

Fine, I thought to myself. If he wanted to bury himself in work instead of addressing our problems, then so be it. I turned on my heel and made my way to the bedroom. The events of the day had taken a toll on me, and my body desperately needed rest.

I really hoped that the champagne would prove expensive enough not to give me a splitting headache in the morning. As I slipped under the blankets, my thoughts returned to the night's events.

For a moment, I contemplated calling my mom. It was late afternoon in Seattle, and she would likely be home. But deep down, I knew she wouldn't fully understand what was going on inside my head and heart. She would simply tell me to stop playing childish games and come back home. With a sigh, I decided to try to get some sleep instead.

To my surprise, sleep came quicker than expected. Tomorrow was a new day. I could deal with the worries then.

Chapter 9

The kiss on the forehead made me stir in bed. I could feel my dream still lingering, with the image of dark chocolate eyes and a captivating smile. "Erica, wake up," a voice whispered, and I opened my eyes, hoping to find Nico when I did. Instead, the sky blue gaze of Tim met mine as he sat at the edge of the bed holding a breakfast tray loaded with coffee, bagels, and a single red rosebud.

"Good morning sleepyhead," Tim smiled.

His gesture caught me off guard. I wasn't sure how to process this sudden change in his behavior. Especially after the argument we had the previous night.

He poured a cup of coffee from the French press and offered it to me.

I remained silent, trying to make sense of it all. Tim cleared his throat, breaking the silence.

"I owe you an apology for yesterday," he began, his tone sincere. I raised an eyebrow, surprised by his admission.

An apology? Well, that was a good start!

"I was a jerk. Work was getting intense, and I took it personally when you didn't reply. I shouldn't have reacted the way I did," Tim confessed, his words tinged with remorse.

I took a moment to process. His work had been consuming him lately, and I understood the pressure he was under. While his apology didn't erase the hurtful things that were said, I realized I couldn't stay mad at him for long.

"I thought I was your best friend," he teased, but his tone turned serious. "You can tell me anything, you know?"

I nodded, acknowledging his statement. But deep down, I knew there were some things I couldn't share with him. My dream of Nico, for instance. It was a reminder of my own fleeting desires, a harmless fantasy that I would keep to myself.

Tim had apologized, and we were making an effort to move past our disagreement. Yet, a part of me wondered if things would truly go back to normal or if there were deeper issues that still needed to be addressed.

The new week rushed in with relentless speed, bringing a tidal wave of work tasks crashing down upon me. Deadlines loomed ominously. Tim seemed genuinely apologetic for his behavior these last few days, and we haven't had any arguments since. However, his long hours at the office, disappearing and returning late at night, left me feeling a twinge of loneliness. I tried to remind myself that supporting his ambitions was important, even if it meant sacrificing some of our quality time together.

Natalia had been feeling guilty for days about Saturday night. I made sure she knows it wasn't her fault. I told her about Tim's surprise breakfast in bed and she seemed to accept that everything was back to normal.

As Friday and the salsa lesson drew near, my emotions grew increasingly conflicted. I found myself torn between the anticipation of seeing Nico again and the fear that he might ask about the supposed emergency that made us leave the club. Those past few days, I didn't bump into him on the staircase. He also didn't appear in my dreams anymore.

Tim did not comment when I was getting ready to leave for salsa class. I appreciated how hard he'd been working to be a better partner. But his reassurance couldn't soothe the inner unrest I felt. It was as if my heart was split in two—each piece heading down a different road — and I couldn't give him all of it anymore.

"Why don't we go out for a nice dinner this weekend?" Tim's voice broke through my internal struggle.

A flicker of genuine happiness tugged at the corner of my lips as I replied, "That'd be lovely, thank you." I wanted to show him that his thoughtfulness mattered, that I still valued our relationship. Come on, Erica, you need to try harder! I embraced Tim tightly, planting a kiss on his cheek before rushing out the door. As I made my way to salsa, I couldn't help but feel a sense of guilt gnawing at me. Tim deserved my full commitment and affection, yet I struggled to push aside the fragments of my heart that yearned for something more.

I arrived at the dance school to find out that Nico was unavailable for the day. Isabelle, his co-teacher, informed us that Armando would take his place. What did "unavailable" mean exactly? Was Nico sick, or was he purposefully avoiding me after our last encounter? I scolded myself for assuming I held any significance in his life. Surely, a confident and attractive guy like Nico wouldn't skip a lesson because of a neighbor girl.

My mind raced, entertaining various possibilities. Maybe he had family drama or a girlfriend occupying his time. The thought of Nico being involved with someone else sent a pang through my stomach. I was surprised how closely my emotions were tied to him.. Each thought of Nico ignited a rollercoaster of sensations within me.

The salsa lesson continued. Roman and Natalia seemed to enjoy themselves, their laughter and chemistry filling the air. I decided to give them some space, hoping that their connection would deepen into something meaningful. Natalia deserved someone who could take care of her and appreciate her remarkable qualities.

Going back, I entered my building. The staircase was quiet. I was hoping to meet Nico walking up the stairs. I imagined him explaining his absence, assuring me he didn't have a girlfriend, and confessing his constant thoughts of me.

But guilt washed over me once again. Tim had been putting in an effort to improve our relationship, and here I was, harboring feelings for another man! I was a terrible girlfriend! I needed to make it up to Tim. Even if he didn't know what I was making up for. Tomorrow I will surprise him at the restaurant looking sexy and we will enjoy each other's company!

"I'll see you at Bebek!" I said cheerfully to Tim over the phone. He had left earlier to drop some documents off at the office. We were set to meet me at the trendy Turkish restaurant later. This gave me a perfect excuse to show up alone and dazzle him with my outfit!

I attempted to recreate the look Natalia gave me last time; it highlighted my cheekbones with perfection and my eyelashes were curled perfectly. I opened my closet, then from its far corner, I pulled out a pair of red pumps that I had brought from Seattle.

Now they were perfect for what I had in mind: pairing them with that little black dress I bought at Bahnhofstrasse, the shopping street, the other day. I got wardrobe envy looking at Natalia's collection. The dress fell in my hands when I was at Modissa. It cost three hundred francs, which is roughly equal to three hundred dollars, but Tim was sure to love it. This dress looked nothing like the one I wore in the Plaza he disliked so much. This one was elegant and when I slipped into the red heels, I felt my legs appeared miles long!

I carefully twisted my hair up into an elegant bun and inspected myself in the mirror, making sure I looked flawless. Then I grabbed my black velvet purse and called an Uber on my phone. There was no way I would attempt to walk any distance in those heels!

As I entered Bebek, a delightful restaurant we had frequented before, I was greeted by the warm smiles of the staff. The hostess complimented me on my appearance, instantly boosting my confidence. As I drew closer to our table, I saw Tim had company. Someone was sitting with him, but his back was turned towards me. A single glance at Tim and his dread was obvious.

"Erica!" Tim exclaimed, springing up from his seat and swiftly draping his jacket around me. I tried to protest, insisting that I didn't need the jacket. Tim seemed insistent, almost forcing me to keep it on. What was going on?

Turning my attention to the man at the table, I recognized him from a family photo. It was Tim's father! Why hadn't Tim mentioned anything about his father joining us? Meeting the family for the first time should have warranted some sort of heads-up, shouldn't it?

The older man rose from his seat and faced me directly. I extended my hand with a trembling voice. "I'm Erica. It's wonderful to finally meet you, Mr. Meier," I said, attempting to maintain composure.

"Pleased to meet you," Tim's father replied in impeccable English. "Call me Horst."

Chapter 10

I took my seat next to Tim, but something was definitely off. My boyfriend's behavior was strange, and his gaze kept fixating on me and my outfit. What was going on?

"So, how is life in Zurich?" Tim's father inquired, breaking the uneasy silence.

"Oh, it's been a bit challenging at first. I still struggle with German, and everything is so new," I began, hoping to steer the conversation away from the tension. Tim let out an audible grunt in response.

"Are you okay?" I asked him, concern filling my voice.

He nodded but remained silent, leaving me even more perplexed.

"So, how are the German lessons going?" Horst continued, trying to keep the conversation flowing.

A blush crept up on my cheeks. "Well, I haven't quite gotten to that point yet. I haven't attended any language classes in Zurich," I confessed, trying to inject a bit of humor into the situation. Unfortunately, my attempt fell flat, and neither of them laughed. It was an awkward moment, to say the least.

"Dad, Erica is taking online lessons. You don't need to physically go to school these days to learn a language," Tim interjected, coming to my rescue.

His father seemed satisfied with the explanation, and I let out a silent sigh of relief. Hopefully, Horst wouldn't delve further into my language-learning progress. The truth was, I had signed up for the classes but never actually attended any. As an English native speaker in Zurich, where many people spoke excellent English, I found little motivation to pursue formal language lessons. However, that was a secret I intended to keep hidden. Horst certainly wouldn't approve.

As the appetizers arrived, we busied ourselves with our salads, dressed with a tangy raspberry and pomegranate dressing. Horst shifted his attention to questioning Tim about his job, granting me a temporary reprieve.

Tim's mother had passed away a few years ago, leaving only Tim and his father. He didn't have any siblings, and their relationship seemed distant. From the snippets Tim had shared, it was clear he had been incredibly close to his mother. His father, always engrossed in work and frequently traveling on business, rarely visited Zurich. It was my first time meeting him in person.

Before the main course arrived, Horst excused himself for a moment, leaving Tim and me alone at the table. Seizing the opportunity, Tim's demeanor shifted, and he hissed at me.

"What are you wearing? And where did those awful shoes come from?" His disapproval pierced through me, making me feel small and inadequate under his judgmental gaze.

"I wanted to surprise you," I replied, struggling to hold back tears. "I thought you'd find me sexy. It would have been nice for you to inform me that your father would be joining us. I would have worn a nun's outfit!"

"We'll discuss it later," he responded, shaking his head, not wanting his father to overhear our conversation.

I was growing weary of this emotional rollercoaster. One moment, Tim was the sweetest guy in the world, and I remembered why I had crossed the ocean for him. The next, something triggered him, and I became his enemy. This inconsistency was not acceptable. I didn't want to cause a scene during my first meeting with his father, but once Horst left, I knew I needed to have a serious conversation with Tim.

Tim's father returned from the bathroom, and I noticed Tim tensing up. He was just as stressed as I was. The pressure to impress his father weighed heavily on him. Tim started talking about his startup again, and I knew this was going to be a long and trying evening.

Thankfully, Horst had booked a room at the Schweizerhof Hotel since we didn't have enough space to host him in our apartment. Tim's father politely said goodnight and I had no idea what he was thinking of me. They planned to meet for brunch, leaving me uncertain about whether I was welcome to join.

Instead of asking Tim to call a taxi, which would surely result in complaints, we took to take the tram. The rest of the way, I endured the discomfort of my shoes without uttering a single complaint. I refused to give Tim the satisfaction of knowing how uncomfortable they were or that I embodied the "spoiled American" stereotype.

During our walk back, Tim kept talking about his father's company. Mr Meier seemed very successful. The pressure for Tim to succeed on his own was undoubtedly intense. At least we were engaged in conversation, avoiding an uncomfortable silence. As we approached our building, the pain in my feet became unbearable, causing me to stop abruptly. Tim, too, halted and looked at me expectantly. I used this moment to address some lingering issues.

"Tim, we need to talk. Properly. I'm not okay with how things have been going these past few weeks," I began, determined to find my inner strength.

Tim glanced around the street dismissively. "We're not going to discuss this here," he scoffed, rolling his eyes. "Let's go home."

"So you can go back to your computer and ignore me again?" I was desperate for him to listen. I took a deep breath, mustering the courage to speak my mind. "You've been acting like a jerk, Tim. We're both busy, but your expectations for our relationship are confusing. Disappearing for hours, overworking yourself, and then dumping all that stress on me—"

"As if you know how to be in a relationship," Tim interjected, cutting me off. "You clearly lack experience. You dress like a desperate single girl craving attention. And salsa? I'm sure it's all Natalia's idea because you'd never come up with something so silly."

"Tim, can't you see what you're doing? Treating me like this won't save our relationship!" I pleaded, tears welling up in my eyes.

Tim snorted and turned on his heel, walking toward our building without waiting for me. I refused to chase after him. Not after his hurtful words and definitely not in these shoes. With a heavy heart, I slowly entered the building. Trying to reason with a man who didn't know how to address conflicts but instead ran from them posed a significant obstacle.

I kicked off my shoes and sat at the bottom step of the staircase. I wasn't ready to face what awaited me inside. I contemplated reaching out to Natalia, but it was late, and she was likely either out or already asleep. I would talk to her tomorrow.

"Good evening," a familiar voice echoed from above. Nico. I quickly wiped away my tears, not wanting him to see me in such a vulnerable state.

He descended the stairs and sat down beside me, momentarily silent as he tried to grasp the situation unfolding before him—me sitting on the stairs with my shoes cast aside.

"You look wonderful," he remarked, his gaze fixed on my face. "But you also look sad. Is everything alright?"

I remained still, unable to form a response.

"Is your boyfriend giving you a hard time?" he asked?

I looked at his face full of concern. So he knew! Well, it wasn't really surprising. Tim's and my names were on the door, and Nico must have seen them when he knocked on our door last time.

A solitary tear clung to the edge of my face, and before it could fall, Nico gently caught it, wiping it away with a tender gesture.

"No woman should cry because of a man," he whispered softly

A sob escaped my mouth. He was so gentle, so empathetic. He lay his hand on the small of my back trying to comfort me. I looked at him, he was so young, yet so remarkably mature.

Slowly, Nico stood up and extended his hand toward me. I gathered my shoes and rose from the steps, following him up the staircase. Tim might come out wondering where I am. That is if he sill cared.

Nico escorted me to the top of the stairs.

"Thank you," I whispered.

Nico smiled and the warmth filled my chest. "If you ever feel like you want to talk, just knock on my door or give me a call," he offered, his voice filled with sincerity.

"But I don't have your number," I hesitated.

Nico winked playfully, his eyes sparkling. "Oh, but you do."

With those mysterious words, he left me standing at the top of the stairs.

Chapter 11

"Are you seriously telling me he saved his phone number on your phone when he showed up at your apartment?!" Natalia's eyes widened in disbelief.

I blushed, feeling a mix of embarrassment and intrigue. "Apparently so," I admitted, unable to suppress a smile. Once Nico said that I already had his number, I dashed into the apartment. I locked myself in the bathroom and started frantically searching my phone for his contact information. And there it was—a mysterious number labeled as "Salsa Teacher." But he wasn't my salsa teacher when he arrived that morning, catching me off guard in my disheveled state. And he must have seen Tim's name on the door, yet he still shared his number with me. Did he find me attractive in that moment, or did he simply perceive me as someone who might need a friend someday, just as I had needed one yesterday? Nico continued to surprise me.

Natalia's expression turned serious, her eyes searching my face for answers. "It's terrible what happened yesterday, though," she said, her tone filled with concern. "How long are you going to let Tim treat you this way?"

I looked down, my heart heavy with the weight of my conflicted emotions. Deep down, I knew that what was happening between Tim and me wasn't healthy. We were falling apart, and yet I kept clinging to excuses and explanations, desperately trying to justify his behavior. I was tormented by guilt over my feelings for another man, as if I were betraying Tim and failing as a partner. I felt like the villain, convinced that I wasn't trying hard enough for him. After all, Tim and I had shared such wonderful moments together, and it was for him I had uprooted my life and moved to a foreign country.

Natalia's question brought me back to reality. "Has he called you yet?"

"Nico? He doesn't have my number," I replied, shaking my head.

"No, darling. Tim," she clarified, her tone emphasizing the significance of her question. "Has he called to apologize for what happened yesterday? You said he was already asleep when you returned to the apartment."

I nodded, memories of Tim being comfortably tucked into bed while I silently slipped back in. It seemed he had found a convenient way to avoid the conflicts at home. But

I was so profoundly affected by my encounter with Nico that I had decided Tim might as well have been asleep.

"Well, he had better." Natalia's voice took on a harsh edge. "Nico was right. There's no way a woman like you should suffer because of a man like Tim."

I spoke, trying to soften the blow of Natalia's words. "Nico didn't exactly put it that way," I started.

"But I am putting it that way," Natalia interjected firmly. "Erica, you need to realize that you're in a toxic relationship, and if Tim doesn't get a grip on himself, he will lose you."

Her words struck a nerve, piercing through the layers of denial I had built around myself. The thought of not being with Tim was unbearable, and the prospect of ending things just a few months into our relationship seemed too drastic. I still loved him, hoping against hope that things would improve between us. And then there was the fear of being alone in a foreign country, with no clear path forward. Moving back to the States was out of the question—I couldn't bear the thought of admitting defeat to my mother. But where would I go? I could hardly move in with Natalia to her tiny flat? I didn't even want to think of the consequences of a failed relationship. The first relationship in a very long time. I needed to get myself together.

Natalia's gaze softened, and she reached out to hold my hand. "Erica, I want nothing more than to see you happy and treated with the love and respect you deserve," she said, her voice gentle yet determined. "I'm here for you, Erica. You're not alone in this. Together, we'll navigate through whatever lies ahead. You deserve love, respect, and a relationship that brings out the best in you."

I came back to an empty apartment. I was relieved this time to have space for myself. I needed some rest after a stressful day at work, and I decided that some yoga in the living room could do wonders. Not that I was practicing yoga much, but that's what everyone always said, didn't they? Yoga and meditation helped to manage your stress and so I decided it was a high time to start.

With closed eyes, I took deep breaths, attempting to find a sense of calm. But as if summoned by my thoughts, Nico's face materialized in my mind—his gentle touch, his comforting gaze. I couldn't help but wonder why he had left his phone number without telling me.

I opened my eyes and grabbed my phone. I opened the contacts list and stared at the 'Salsa Teacher' record and the number below. I hesitated to make the call, but the idea of leaving a message felt more within my comfort zone. It was a direct line to Nico, away from the watchful eyes of his class or the prying gazes of the club. A chance to hide behind the safety of a written message.

I typed out a simple "*Hi* " and pressed send. Almost instantly, the familiar checkmarks appeared, showing that the message had been delivered. Setting the phone aside, I attempted to return to my meditation, but it buzzed to life again, interrupting my focus.

Hello Erica, feeling better?

Nico's reply appeared on the screen, accompanied by an upside-down smiley. It was a small gesture, but it made me smile too.

Yes, thank you. And thank you for yesterday.

I replied. *Happy to help. Any time you need cheering up, I'm here.* He responded, adding a playful wink.

That's good to know. I added a smiling face.

Are you home? Nico asked.

Yes. I replied. My curiosity piqued as to where this conversation was leading.

Almost immediately, a new message appeared. *Alone?* He asked.

Strange thing was happening in my stomach. Butterflies danced in my stomach initially, but a wave of unease quickly overtook them. Should I tell the truth? What did Nico have in mind if I admitted to being alone? Should I play along with this game? Conflicting thoughts battled in my mind.

After a moment of hesitation, I responded with a simple, "Yes." I pressed send, my heart pounding. I waited for him to message back right away. But as time stretched on without a response, I let out a disappointed sigh, berating myself for getting carried away. Perhaps he was simply engaging in small talk, being friendly. Determined to shift my focus, I stood up, adjusted my purple leggings and pink gym top, and decided to indulge in some yoga.

Just as I settled into a pose, my phone vibrated. I lunged for it, fingers fumbling to unlock the screen. After a few failed attempts, it prompted me to wait thirty seconds or input my password. Hastily entering the password, I opened the messaging app.

I'll be home late. Having dinner with Dad before he goes back to Geneva. The message flashed across the screen, startling me for a moment. It was from Tim, not Nico. I sighed, realizing that Nico had yet to respond. With a resigned acceptance, I typed a brief '*OK*' in reply to Tim. The encounter with Horst hadn't been particularly successful, and I supposed Tim would prefer to handle his father on his own.

Frustrated, I tossed my phone onto the sofa and made my way to the kitchen to get some water. It got hot for a moment and it wasn't thanks to the exercise.

I heard a knock on the door. My heart skipped a beat and I almost choke on the water. It couldn't be him, could it?

I hurried to the door and swung it open wide, revealing Nico standing before me. He seemed somewhat bashful, uncertain if it was appropriate for him to come over. His eyes darted over my shoulder, checking the surroundings inside my apartment, as if confirming that Tim was indeed absent. My happiness surged at the sight of him. I suppose I couldn't expect him to keep texting me when he lived just next door.

I gazed at him, waiting for him to say something, to explain his unexpected visit.

"Would you like to practice some salsa?" His arm gestured toward his apartment, an invitation hanging in the air.

Chapter 12

I stood there, contemplating Nico's invitation. The idea of joining him for a salsa lesson in the comfort of his home tugged at my curiosity, but it also sparked a twinge of hesitation. There were so many "what ifs" swirling in my mind. What if Tim unexpectedly returned home and saw me leaving Nico's apartment? What if being in such proximity to Nico ignited a spark that I couldn't resist? And most importantly, what if I allowed myself to enjoy the evening a little too much?

Sensing my internal struggle, Nico patiently waited, his kind eyes fixed on me. There was a gentle reassurance in his gaze, as if he understood the battle I was fighting within myself.

"Come on," he said, a hint of a smile playing on his lips. "It will cheer you up, I promise."

I took a deep breath, trying to steady the vertigo of thoughts inside my head. An extra salsa lesson couldn't hurt, right? It was just an innocent activity, a chance to improve my dancing skills. That was the excuse I clung to, desperately trying to convince myself that it was a harmless adventure, nothing more.

"Alright," I finally agreed, making a conscious decision to silence the nagging voice of doubt within me. I reached for the door handle, only to be reminded by Nico's playful remark, "Don't lock yourself out."

I blushed as I realized how easily I could have forgotten my keys! Imagining the embarrassing scenario of having to call Tim to explain the reason made me chuckle nervously. I quickly retrieved my keys and followed Nico as we descended the stairs.

I wondered what Nico's apartment looked like. When I first met him, he seemed like an ordinary guy with probably a typical apartment. But then, I caught a glimpse of him at the Plaza, dressed impeccably, mingling effortlessly in the VIP section. It left me pondering what surprises his place might hold.

As we made our way to his apartment, a mixture of nervousness and curiosity swirled within me. What awaited me in this impromptu salsa session? Would it be like the classes we had attended, or would it be a more intimate setting, amplifying the intensity between us? I tried to push those thoughts aside, reminding myself that this was solely about dancing and nothing more.

Entering Nico's apartment, the inviting ambiance struck me. Soft music floated through the air, setting the perfect atmosphere for a dance session. A large mirror adorned one wall, reflecting the warmth of the dimmed lights and creating an illusion of infinite space. It was the same size as ours but much brighter. He was surely getting more sunlight here. The apartment was decorated with a taste. Vibrant artwork hanging on the walls captured the essence of Latin culture. Dark furniture was combined well with an indigo velvet sofa. There were golden accents everywhere making it look cozy but stylish at the same time.

"I love your apartment!" I exclaimed, glancing around the beautifully designed space.

"Thank you," Nico replied with a warm smile. "A friend of mine, an interior designer, did all of this."

My heart sank a little. He mentioned a woman—a friend who had played a role in decorating his apartment. Was there someone special in his life, someone he entrusted with such personal choices? Nico seemed oblivious to the impact his words had on me. He guided me towards the kitchen, offering me a drink. He casually instructed Alexa to play Latin music in the background.

I reminded myself to stay present, focusing on the fact that it was me he had invited here. I was the one by his side now, not his decorator friend.

"So, where were you during the last salsa lesson?" I asked nonchalantly, trying to keep the conversation flowing.

Nico's eyes darkened, hinting at a hidden weight. "I had a personal matter to take care of," he replied, offering no further explanation.

Was it a woman or something else entirely? I decided not to pry any further; there was already enough going on in my own life to worry about. Instead, I chose to embrace the present moment and enjoy his company.

Thankfully, Nico's mood quickly brightened. "Never mind all that!" he exclaimed, grinning. "You can enjoy the luxury of a private lesson now."

He extended his hand, leading me to the living room. A rush of excitement coursed through me, though it wasn't solely about salsa. Yes, I still felt like I had two left feet, but the thrill of being alone with Nico, having him all to myself, resurrected those butterflies in my stomach.

He pulled me closer, commanding Alexa to turn up the music, and we began going through the basic steps.

"Remember, the fourth one is just a tap," he instructed. "You don't shift your body weight on the tap."

Nico's patience was unwavering as I struggled to follow his guidance. I grew increasingly frustrated with myself.

"Look at me, Erica," he said, halting my gaze from the fixating on my feet. I was too focused on controlling every move.

I locked eyes with him, attempting to let go and relax. *Don't overthink it*, I reminded myself. *This is supposed to be fun, not work.*

"Ready?" Nico asked, a mischievous glint in his eyes. "I'll count to three, and then we start again. One, two—"

Just as Nico said, "Two," he made his move, catching me off guard. We immediately fell into a seamless flow. It was a clever trick on his part, knowing that I would be anticipating the count of three and overthinking my every move. The pace quickened, and he effortlessly spun me around my own axis. The exhilaration of it all made me laugh like a carefree little girl, surrendering myself to his lead as he whisked me across his living room floor.

The music swelled, enveloping us in its pulsating rhythm, and Nico's cheeky grin only grew wider. We were fully immersed in the vibrant embrace of salsa. His touch was both firm and gentle, guiding me through each step with unwavering precision and graceful elegance. Our bodies moved as one, perfectly synchronized, and the electric energy between us became palpable.

It was fun. It was more fun than I had in a long time. He helped me let go. I could be myself not thinking if anyone was watching me. As we danced, a sense of liberation washed over me. The worries and doubts that had plagued my mind began to fade, replaced by the sheer joy of movement and connection. In that moment, it didn't matter what could happen or what others might think. All that mattered was the exhilaration of the present, the raw emotions channeled through the vibrant dance.

Nico's infectious laughter filled the room as we stumbled through a particularly challenging sequence. "Don't worry," he reassured me. "It's all about letting go and enjoying the journey. Mistakes are part of the process."

His words resonated within me, not just in terms of dancing, but in life as well. It was a reminder that sometimes, it's okay to take risks, to let go of the fear of what might happen. Life is about embracing the unexpected, learning from our missteps, and finding joy in the present moment.

Nico pushed the top of my body backwards towards the floor and pull me quickly back in, our faces just an inch from each other. I could feel his warm breath on my skin and his eyes were even darker than I remembered. Our gazes locked, and for a brief moment, time seemed to stand still. He looked at me as if he was going to kiss me here and now. I didn't have time to consider what we're doing. The music finished and Nico took a step back.

"Well, it wasn't so bad, was it?" he tried to joke, but he was as flushed as I was. He walked towards the kitchen, leaving me alone. I felt kind of robbed of the moment we could have had. But was it such a good idea to try anything when, in fact, I lived upstairs with my boyfriend?

"I should go," I said, with a hint of apprehension. It was the wise thing to do, even if it felt like I was leaving behind something valuable and worthwhile. Avoiding temptation was important to maintain my relationship and self-respect..

Nico, ever the gentleman, offered me a glass of water with a gesture that both expressed his sympathy and comforted me. I gratefully accepted and took a sip, allowing it to give me a brief break from my chaotic thoughts and feelings.

"Thank you for the lesson," I managed to say, my voice filled with a blend of gratitude and regret. With a heavy sigh, I turned and made my way out of his apartment, acutely aware of the door closing behind me, sealing off the tantalizing world I had just glimpsed.

"See you on Friday, Erica," Nico called out, his voice carrying a hint of longing that mirrored my own conflicted feelings. I nodded, unable to bring myself to meet his gaze, and walked back to the familiarity of my apartment.

Chapter 13

I shut the door and rested my head against its cold surface, trying to take comfort in the stillness of the room. My heart rate was still elevated, memories of the music and hidden cravings lingered with me. I knew this was a turning point, an indication that our decisions shape who we are.

I knew that I had made the right decision, that integrity and faithfulness were the foundations on which love was built. Yet, a part of me couldn't help but wonder what could have been. The forbidden allure of Nico's embrace lingered in my mind.

I took a deep breath, determined to push aside the lingering temptation and focus on the commitment I had made to Tim. It was time to reaffirm my devotion and to navigate the complexities of my emotions with honesty and integrity.

With a renewed sense of purpose, I stepped away from the door. Ready to confront the challenges that lay ahead, I opened my laptop and started my research. I wanted to try yet again to meet Tim halfway. This time, I was going to surprise him with something I knew he'd enjoy. I would book a hotel in the Alps that he liked. I will try to reignite the fire we had in the beginning. I will try to have the kind of attraction with Tim that I just had with Nico.

Seeing the way he Nico reacted to my question before, his situation appeared complicated. There probably was a woman in the mix that he hadn't mentioned. It wasn't worth trying to interfere in his life when I had a relationship with Tim. That was what required my attention right now. I kept repeating these words of wisdom to myself as a way to drown out the small voice inside me. It was urging me to find a way to end things with Tim. As usual, I held onto my stubbornness and refused to give up so easily.

Pages upon pages of hotels, resorts, and mountain retreats filled my screen. Each promising a unique experience amidst breathtaking natural beauty. I meticulously read through reviews, compared prices, and evaluated amenities, searching for the ideal setting to whisk Tim away to. I wanted this trip to be unforgettable, to remind him of the passion and adventure we had once shared. Money didn't matter.

As the reservation confirmation appeared on my screen, I felt the excitement filling me again. I couldn't wait to surprise Tim! To show him that despite the challenges we faced, my love and commitment remained unwavering. It was time to put in the work, to nurture our relationship, and to create new memories that would solidify our bond.

I closed my laptop, feeling a renewed sense of purpose and determination. It wasn't going to be easy, but love rarely is. I was prepared to meet the challenges head-on. I was armed with the knowledge that relationships require effort, understanding, and a willingness to grow.

Tim's eyes widened with surprise as he caught sight of the confirmation email on my laptop screen. "You booked a hotel in Zermatt?" he exclaimed, a hint of excitement in his voice.

I smiled, feeling a surge of relief. "Yes, I thought it would be a wonderful surprise for you. A chance to escape the city and reconnect."

He approached me, wrapping his arms around my waist. "You have no idea how much I needed this," he whispered, his warm breath grazing my ear. "Thank you, Erica. I can't wait to go."

As the days passed, our anticipation grew. Friday afternoon, we stood at the bustling train station, ready to begin our journey. The sun's golden rays illuminated the platform and Tim seemed to be in a great mood. I have skipped my salsa lesson and give all my time to him.

With our backpacks slung over our shoulders, we boarded the train, finding a cozy spot by the window. As the train moved, Tim and I gazed out at the passing landscapes, marveling at the breathtaking beauty of the Swiss countryside.

As we journeyed towards the Alps, I noticed a newspaper lying on the seat beside me. The headline caught my attention: "The Rise of the Romero Family: Colombian Tycoons Conquer Zurich."

Curiosity piqued, I began reading the article. It detailed the remarkable success of the Romero family, who had recently made Zurich their new home. From real estate investments to thriving businesses, they seemed to have an uncanny knack for turning ventures into gold. There were some pictures of the Romero senior and his wife at some posh restaurant. In the article, there was a mention of three sons they had but no pictures.

Fascinated, I shared the article with Tim. "Look at this. The Romeros. They've achieved so much here. It's inspiring."

Tim skimmed the article, nodding thoughtfully. "It just goes to show that with the right opportunities and determination, anything is possible."

As we continued our journey, our conversation shifted towards our expectations for the weekend getaway. Tim promised to leave his laptop behind and fully immerse himself in our time together. He vowed to disconnect from work and devote his attention to us.

I felt a glimmer of hope, a belief that perhaps this trip could be a turning point for us. I yearned to bring our relationship back to the place it once was, where love overflowed and the spark between us burned bright.

Yet, the image of Nico lingered in my mind. I battled with the conflicting emotions that surged within me. I loved Tim, but the magnetic pull towards Nico was undeniable. It was a forbidden attraction that clawed at my heart, testing the boundaries of my loyalty.

As we arrived at the picturesque hotel nestled in the heart of the Alps, I decided to focus on repairing things with Tim.

Our room overlooked a breathtaking vista of snow-capped peaks, stretching as far as the eye could see.

As the sun dipped below the horizon, we sat on the balcony watching the sunset.

"I want to thank you, Erica," Tim spoke breaking the silence. "This trip is exactly what I need. What we need. I've realized how much I've been neglecting us."

Gratitude washed over me. Tim recognized the effort I had put into planning this weekend away!

"I'm glad it meant something to you," I replied, my voice filled with a hint of longing. "I've missed us, missed the connection we used to have."

Tim's gaze softened, and he reached for my hand, intertwining our fingers. "I know I've been distant lately, caught up in the demands of work. But being here with you has reminded me of what truly matters."

I wanted to believe his words, to cling to the hope that we could rebuild what we had lost. Yet, deep down, a gnawing doubt remained. I couldn't shake the image of Tim's laptop, the constant presence that seemed to overshadow our moments together.

We spent Saturday hiking, relaxing at the resort spa, and enjoying each other's company. I even promised to go jogging the next day to prove my commitment. In the evening, we were getting ready to go to the resort's restaurant for an early dinner. It was meant to be a special occasion, a chance to savor our time together. Or so I thought. As we stepped into the elegant dining room, my heart sank.

We bumped into two men who introduced themselves as Tim's sponsors. They greeted Tim and smiled at me. One man pointed at the table by the window and said they'll be waiting for us there. As soon as they walked away,

I forced a smile, trying to mask my disappointment. "Tim, you never mentioned they would be here."

He stammered, attempting to gather his thoughts. "I... I didn't know they would be here either. Must be a coincidence."

But deep down, I knew it wasn't a coincidence. Tim's inability to truly leave work behind had brought his investors into our sanctuary, invading the space we had hoped to reclaim.

Feeling a mix of anger and hurt, I stayed for the appetizer. Before the main meal arrived, I excused myself from the table, citing a sudden headache. I needed to escape, to process the emotions crashing through me. As I retreated to our room, I reached for my phone, finding a text message waiting for me.

It was from Nico.

Hey, Erica. I noticed you weren't at salsa yesterday. Everything okay?

I had skipped the salsa lesson to be with Tim, to dedicate this weekend to us. But now, I faced the consequences of that choice. I hesitated, unsure of how to respond.

With a deep breath, I replied, *Sorry, Nico. I had something come up and couldn't make it. Hope it went well.*

Almost instantly, a reply appeared, and my heart quickened in anticipation.

No worries. We missed your energy, though. Let me know if you're free for the next lesson.

I paused, my fingers hovering over the keyboard. The temptation to explore the connection I felt with Nico was strong. But I had committed myself to Tim, and I couldn't betray that trust.

I typed. *I'll let you know. Thanks, Nico.*

Setting my phone aside, I let out a sigh. The conflicting emotions within me raged on. It was a battle I couldn't ignore.

Tim wasn't back until it was late. He muttered 'sorry' and 'goodnight' and turned over, falling asleep instantly. I could smell alcohol on his breath.

As the night grew quiet, the weight of the decisions I had made settled upon me. I longed for the love and passion Tim and I shared not long ago. Now looking at him asleep, I felt less and less attraction towards this man. I couldn't deny the pull towards Nico, the allure of a connection that felt both forbidden and undeniable.

Closing my eyes, I whispered a silent plea for the universe to help me see the right way. The way to a happy relationship. The way to feel loved and accepted.

Chapter 14

The morning sunlight streamed through the window, casting a soft glow on the room as I carefully folded my clothes and placed them in my suitcase. Zermatt had lost its charm overnight, tainted by the disappointment and realization that our weekend getaway hadn't brought the desired changes in our relationship.

Tim watched me silently, his brows furrowed with a mix of concern and frustration. "Erica, are you sure about this? We still have the train tickets for the evening. It's a waste of money to leave early."

I paused, my hands gripping the edge of the suitcase. He was really testing me. I knew I couldn't stay here any longer.

"I need to go home, Tim," I said, my voice tinged with sadness. "I need some time to think, to figure things out."

His expression hardened, and I could see the offense in his eyes. "So you're just going to leave me here? We still have the whole day at the hotel. It was a dinner for god's sake!"

Tears welled up in my eyes, and I took a step closer to him, reaching out to touch his arm. "Tim, I've been trying. We both have. But sometimes, it's not enough. We need more than just empty gestures and temporary fixes. We need real change."

He pulled away, shaking his head. "You're being unfair, Erica. I thought this weekend meant something to you."

A pang of guilt shot through me, but I couldn't let it sway my decision. I needed to prioritize my own well-being and happiness. I shook my head, kissed him on the cheek and left without saying anything more.

As I made my way to the train station, the weight of my choices settled upon me. Natalia, my loyal friend, was waiting on the platform. Her eyes held a mixture of concern and anger as she embraced me.

"Erica, what happened? I can see it in your eyes. He hurt you, didn't he?" she said, her voice laced with protectiveness.

My voice was caught in my throat. "Things didn't go as planned. I thought this weekend would bring us closer, but instead, it highlighted the cracks in our relationship."

She squeezed my hand, offering me a small smile. "Sometimes, the cracks can't be fixed, Erica. You deserve happiness, and if Tim can't give that to you, then maybe it's time to reassess your situation."

Her words resonated within me, stirring a mix of determination and fear. I had invested so much in this relationship, and the thought of starting over seemed daunting. But deep down, I knew Natalia was right. It was time to seriously think about what I wanted.

We spent the day together in my apartment, talking and sharing our thoughts. Natalia listened attentively, offering support and guidance as I poured my heart out. She painted my nails as we relaxed with face masks on, reminding me of the importance of looking after myself and finding comfort in being around a dependable friend.

As the day wore on, Natalia prepared to leave, her eyes filled with concern. "Erica, promise me you'll think about what I've said. Don't let yourself be trapped in a toxic relationship. You deserve so much more."

I nodded, gratitude swelling in my chest. "I promise, Natalia. I'll take some time to reflect and make the right decision for myself."

Alone in the apartment, I found myself wrestling with my thoughts. I needed an escape, a respite from the tumultuous emotions swirling inside me. With hesitation, I reached for my phone and dialed Nico's number. My heart yearned to hear his voice.

After a few rings, instead of Nico's voice, a woman answered the phone. The sound of her laughter echoed through the line, sending a shiver down my spine.

"Who is this?" she asked with a Latin accent.

I hung up. She asked who I was. Didn't Nico save my number? Who was she? What was her relationship with Nico? I felt betrayed, and the emotions, fueled by my imagination, spiraled out of control.

Before I could gather my wits, Tim arrived home, exhaustion etched on his face. He placed his luggage on the wooden floor in the hall, kicked his shoes into the corner and approached me cautiously.

"Erica, can we talk? I want to understand why you're so distant." His voice was gentle. He placed his hand on my arm and squeezed it slightly.

But this time, I didn't want to talk. I was fed up with the constant turmoil and uncertainty that had consumed my life. The events of the day had left me exhausted and drained.

"I can't, Tim," I said, my voice weary. "I need to go to bed. I'm exhausted."

Tim's brows furrowed, and he reached out a hand as if to touch my arm. "But Erica, we can't just ignore this. We need to talk it out, and find a way forward."

I shook my head, my voice tinged with frustration. "No, Tim. We've had countless conversations that led us nowhere. Right now, all I want is some rest."

Disappointment clouded his features, but he relented. "Alright, if that's what you need. But promise me we'll talk in the morning."

I nodded, silently acknowledging his request, though deep down, I wasn't sure if I had the strength for another discussion that would only lead to more empty promises.

My mind was spinning. The questions about the woman who had answered Nico's phone consumed my every waking moment. Why hadn't Nico texted me afterwards? Was there something going on between them? The possibilities taunted me, causing my imagination to run wild.

Sleep eluded me, and I tossed and turned in the bed, my thoughts drifting between anger, confusion, and longing. I yearned for the peacefulness of the past, the simplicity of my relationship with Tim before it became entangled in doubt and mistrust.

The night dragged on, and when the first rays of morning light peeked through the curtains, I knew I couldn't delay the inevitable any longer. It was time to confront the tangled mess of my life head-on.

As Tim stirred awake beside me, his eyes filled with hope, I took a deep breath and mustered the courage to speak my truth. "Tim, we need to talk, but not now. I need some time alone to gather my thoughts and make sense of everything."

He reached out a hand, his voice filled with desperation. "Please, Erica, don't shut me out. I love you, and I want to work through this together."

A pang of sadness echoed within me, but I knew that love alone wasn't enough to sustain a relationship. I had to find my own happiness, to rediscover the person I had lost along the way.

"I can't keep living in this state of uncertainty, Tim," I said, my voice steady but tinged with sorrow. "I need clarity, and right now, that means taking a step back."

Tim's eyes welled up with tears, and he nodded, defeated. "If that's what you think is best... I won't stop you. Just know that I'll be here, waiting for you."

I couldn't bring myself to respond, my heart heavy with the weight of our broken connection. As I gathered my belongings and walked out of the room, leaving Tim behind, I knew that this was a pivotal moment, one that would shape the trajectory of my future.

The door closed behind me, and I found myself standing on the threshold, facing the unknown. Natalia's words echoed in my mind, reminding me of my worth and the importance of finding happiness.

Chapter 15

Natalia opened the door, her hair wrapped in a towel. One look at my face and at the luggage I have been holding, and she announced: "We're calling in sick!"

She took my stuff, placed them in her bedroom, and wrapped her arms around me. That's when the dam holding everything inside of me broke. The tears were streaming down my face; I was sobbing. My face got all puffy and eyes swollen. It didn't matter. Natalia held me until I cried out about everything I had in me. When the loud sobs turned into a slight hiccup, she stood up and returned from the kitchen, handing me a glass.

I took a big gulp and almost spat it all out on the floor. "I thought it was water!"

Natalia shrugged. "You need something stronger."

"It's eight in the morning!"

"Where I come from, vodka is a remedy for a broken heart. At least a temporary one."

I took a sip and let the liquid burn my throat. I did feel better.

Natalia looked at me with concern. "How are you feeling? Ready to talk about it?"

I nodded. I told her about my weekend in Zermatt. Natalia was a wonderful friend. She scoffed at the right moments. Her eyes were wide in disbelief when I told her about Tim's investors. Them crashing our romantic weekend and she cried "no!" when I told her about a woman answering Nico's phone.

When I finished my story, Natalia cleared her throat and shifted her weight on the sofa. "I might know who the woman was—"

"How?" I was shocked.

"During the salsa class, I noticed a woman standing outside the door. She looked angry and impatient. At first I thought she was waiting for the next lesson, but then she banged on the door and Nico left the room to talk to her."

"Have you seen her before?" I asked, hoping to get more information.

Natalia shook her head. "No idea who that was. They talked for a few minutes and Nico came back in. He didn't look happy." Natalia grabbed my hand. "Sorry, I'm only telling you this now. I didn't want to interrupt your weekend with Tim. You were supposed to rebuild your bond and mentioning Nico didn't seam to be a great idea."

I nodded. "Of course, I understand."

"She was ugly," Natalia said.

I chuckled. She was such a good friend. "Thank you, but I can't believe that!"

"Fine, she was pretty." Natalia rolled her eyes. "But you're much more beautiful! She was definitely older than Nico."

"Well, I guess that's his type," I sighed. "Did she wait for him?"

"She was gone after that heated conversation."

"Probably waiting for him at his place," I grimaced.

Natalia embraced me and stroke my head. "Darling, we don't know who that was. For all we know, it was a psycho ex he wanted to get rid of."

I let out another loud sigh. "Men make us crazy."

Natalia nodded in agreement, her voice filled with empathy. "They certainly have a way of driving us up the wall. But remember, not all men are the same. You deserve someone who cherishes you and treats you with the respect you deserve."

I mustered a weak smile, grateful for Natalia's words of comfort. "Thank you. I needed to hear that."

We sat in silence for a moment, the weight of the situation still lingering in the air.

"Natalia, what should I do now?" I asked.

She took a sip of vodka from my glass. She didn't even wince. "First, take some time for yourself. Heal and process everything that has happened. Rediscover your own worth and what you truly want in a relationship. And when you're ready, confront Tim and have an open, honest conversation about your feelings and concerns."

I nodded, absorbing her advice. It made sense to focus on self-reflection and self-care before taking any further steps.

Natalia squeezed my hand, her eyes filled with determination. "Remember, you have the strength to make the right decisions for yourself. Don't let anyone else dictate your happiness."

It surprised me how wise her words were. "Girl, why are you still single? Everyone would be lucky to have you!"

Natalia sighed. "I guess I haven't found the one who makes me happy yet."

"And Roman? How is it going?" I felt bad for focusing on my heartaches, forgetting that she, like many single women in the city, was struggling to find love.

"It's going well, but I'm following my grandma's advice," she said.

"What advice?" I was curious.

"Grandma always said you can only show one butt cheek to a man, never both."

I laughed out loud. "What on earth does that mean?"

"Well, if you show them both, they lose interest," she explained. "Which means for now I'm being careful giving too much."

I nodded. Grandma's wisdom was timeless.

Natalia and I spent the entire day together, indulging in a much-needed break from reality. We watched silly movies, danced around the living room, and sang along to our favorite songs at the top of our lungs. The weight of the world slowly lifted from my shoulders as laughter filled the air.

In between bouts of giggles and heartfelt conversations, Natalia reminded me of my worth and strength. She encouraged me to embrace the journey of self-discovery and to let go of the past that no longer served me. Her unwavering support and lightheartedness gave me the courage to face the challenges that lay ahead.

"I'm lucky to have you in my life," I said when we sat on the balcony eating pizza we ordered. "You've been my rock through all of this."

She laughed softly, her eyes sparkling. "The feeling is mutual, darling. Now, let's focus on moving forward and finding your inner peace. And if that means another glass of 'remedy' later on, I won't judge."

I laughed. She was fun to be around. Caring, patient, energetic. She knew exactly how to take my mind off the two men that bothered my heart right now.

I left my phone in my handbag the whole day. I knew if I had it next to me I'd be keep checking whether a message arrived. I wasn't sure whom I wanted to hear more from right now. Tim, saying he really understood what losing me meant. Or Nico, telling me that the woman on the phone meant nothing and that he couldn't stop thinking about me.

Natalia said goodnight, saying she needed her beauty sleep. I remained on the balcony, captivated by the tranquility that settled over Zurich. The city gradually transitioned into a quieter state. Fewer people strolling the streets and the hum of public transport diminishing.

I leaned against the balcony railing, taking in the serene view before me. The city lights twinkled like stars scattered across the landscape, casting a gentle glow that danced upon the calm waters of the nearby river. As I turned to head back inside, a bright star caught my eye, shining in the night sky. It reminded me that even in the darkest moments, there was always a flicker of light guiding us forward.

Chapter 16

The following days were a turmoil of work, deadlines, and meetings. Immersed in the familiar chaos of my professional life, I found refuge in the demanding tasks that kept my mind occupied. The challenges and responsibilities served as a temporary distraction from the complexities of my heart.

"You can stay with me as long as you need," Natalia offered. "If you're not sure whether to give Tim another chance, there's no point looking for a new place."

Her generosity and understanding were constant reminders that I was not alone on this journey. This lifted the weight off my shoulders. I had the freedom to decide what I wanted to do without stressing about it. I didn't want to overstay my welcome, but I needed this time to get myself together. I also stopped going to salsa. If I were to decide what I wanted, I needed to distance myself from both men.

One sunny afternoon, as I took a break from work and enjoyed a leisurely lunch in a nearby park, my phone buzzed with a text message. It was Tim.

Are you ready to talk?

The temptation to reply was strong, but something inside me urged me to leave it unanswered. I knew deep down that focusing on myself and my own healing was paramount at this moment.

I took a stroll through the park, feeling the warmth of the sun on my skin and the gentle breeze brushing against my face. The peaceful serenity of the surroundings helped to calm my restless mind, if only for a while.

But as fate would have it, my peace was short-lived. As I was getting closer to the picnic area, the music grew louder. From a distance, I noticed a familiar silhouette. Nico, looking more handsome than I remembered, was accompanied by some friends, one of them - a beautiful Latin woman. They were laughing and dancing. Zurich can be so small! My heart sank as I watched them, the sight triggering a pang of jealousy within me. Was she the woman I heard on the phone? Was she the same one that showed up at the dance school?

Nico, as if sensing me staring, turned around and his gaze met mine from afar. The butterflies exploded in my stomach again, but one more look at the woman standing next to him brought all the feelings I was struggling with over the past days. Nico tried to make his way toward me, calling out my name. But the ache in my heart propelled me to turn and walk away, unwilling to confront the complex emotions that threatened to overwhelm me. I didn't want to cry in front of him again. I still remembered his tender embrace while dancing in his apartment. I longed for affection, but I was stubborn.

Few days turned into two weeks. Tim had surprisingly kept his distance since his last message. Nico and I hadn't crossed our paths. As the days wore on, I found myself running out of clean clothes and underwear. The situation had become dire, and I decided it was time to retrieve some more of my belongings from the apartment I shared with Tim.

"I'm going to go to the apartment and grab some more stuff. Are you sure you're okay with me staying a few more days?" I asked Natalia.

She laughed, her eyes sparkling with amusement. "Girl, you're doing me a favor! If it weren't for you, I'd probably bring Roman here already. You keep me strong in my resolve."

I rolled my eyes playfully and chuckled. "I'm glad things are going well, Natalia. You truly deserve it!"

I left her place and hopped onto a tram that would take me back to the apartment I shared with Tim. I was confident he had already left for the office, allowing me to sneak in unnoticed. I turned the key in the lock and opened the door cautiously. The apartment was quiet, neat and tidy, with the lingering scent of freshly brewed coffee in the air. It seemed I had just missed Tim. Lucky save!

Taking a moment to gather my thoughts, I sank into the familiar comfort of the living room. It was the space I had called home for the past few months, but now, doubts crept into my mind. Did I truly want to come back here? Could Tim and I develop a meaningful and deep connection despite our differences?

Sighing, I pushed those thoughts aside and focused on the task at hand. I rummaged through my belongings, gathering clothes and cosmetics, feeling a mixture of sadness and relief. I knew I had to leave, even if temporarily, for the sake of my own happiness and clarity.

Once I had everything I needed packed into a sports bag, I stood by the front door, ready to leave. As if déjà vu, I saw Nico waiting at my door. The scenes of the past weeks flashed before my eyes. The first encounter, me frantically holding my towel, salsa lessons, the night at the club, Nico's apartment, the woman's voice in the receiver, them in the park...

"What are you doing here, Nico?" I asked, my voice guarded.

"I needed to see you," he replied, his eyes filled with concern. "I wanted to know if you're okay."

I hesitated, unsure of whether engaging in a conversation with him would bring me closer to healing or simply deepen the wounds. But there was an undeniable magnetic pull, an irresistible force that drew me towards him.

"I don't think it's a good idea, Nico," I said, my voice trembling slightly. "We both know it's complicated."

He took a step closer, his gaze unwavering. "I don't care about complications, I just wanted to see you, to make sure you're alright."

Against my better judgment, I nodded reluctantly. "Fine. Let's talk," I relented.

Nico's face softened, relief evident in his eyes. We walked side by side, the tension between us palpable yet unspoken. Silence hung in the air, heavy with unspoken words and unresolved feelings.

Finally, Nico broke the silence. "I haven't seen you around here for a while. You stopped coming to salsa. Have I done something?"

I pondered how to explain what was going in my heart. I wasn't ready to be this vulnerable. "I had some personal matters to take care of." I used the same explanation Nico did last time we talked.

"Anything I can help you with?" he asked, his gaze sincere and caring.

I dismissed his question with a subtle shake of my head. "How have you been?"

Nico stopped, his eyes locked with mine. I saw he was no fool. We were tip toeing around our feelings, but the attraction was tangible. I attempted to guard my heart, wary of the consequences of surrendering to the emotions that swirled within me. Yet, in Nico's presence, resistance felt futile.

"Erica..." he began, his voice filled with a mix of hesitation and longing.

"Yes?" I replied, my heart pounding in my chest, the anticipation almost unbearable.

"I can't stop thinking about you," he confessed.

I felt as if the lightning struck me. I stood there hearing the words I was yearning to hear, but never thought I would.

Nico continued. "I know it's wrong. I know you have a boyfriend. But since the moment I saw you, I couldn't get you out of my head."

I stood there, rooted to the ground, my mind racing as a thousand thoughts collided. This was what I yearned to hear, the validation of the connection I felt. But life wasn't a fairytale, and relationships were never simple.

"I'm so sorry!" Nico grabbed my hand, his touch electric and comforting at the same time. "I didn't want to spring this upon you! I... I thought maybe you felt the same."

I thought of Tim. Of all those evenings where he left me alone. The moments when I didn't feel good enough for him. And then I looked at Nico being so wonderful since the moment I met him. But was it something more than an attraction? Was it worth starting something when the relationship I had didn't exactly end yet? His life was clearly complicated. Another woman.

I wasn't ready for this. I wasn't ready to make a decision that could change my life drastically.

"Nico, I..." I stammered, my voice choked with emotions.

But he interrupted me, releasing my hand with a mixture of understanding and disappointment. "Shall we walk back?" he suggested, masking his own pain.

I nodded. "Please don't be mad at me, Nico," I pleaded, my voice laced with regret.

"You don't need to say more. I completely understand," he reassured me, his tone tinged with sorrow.

We walked back to our building in silence, the weight of unspoken words hanging heavily between us. I couldn't bring myself to tell him I no longer lived here. As we reached the entrance, I waited for Nico to disappear into his apartment before hurrying away, my heart heavy with the weight of what could have been. The temptation to knock on Nico's door and seek refuge in his arms was overwhelming, but I knew it wouldn't solve anything. Relationships were messy, complicated, and I needed time to sort through my own feelings before making any decisions.

Chapter 17

As the days unfolded, I found escape in the quiet moments, immersing myself in the books that transported me to distant places. It certainly did me well to have some time to myself. To be able to breathe and relax. Not having to engage in disagreements. Not being taunted by feelings for Nico that kept surfacing when he was near. I was particularly fond of romance novels, with their tales of true love conquering all. Reality wasn't as forgiving, but while immersed in its pages, I could pretend that it was. Why couldn't life be more like the stories?

In romance novels, there was always a happy ending; the sweet taste of success overcoming any obstacles in the way. Even when it seemed all was lost, I knew that if I kept reading, I would find out how things worked out in the end. Every page provided an opportunity to get lost in a world with no limits and expectations. It was a chance to imagine possibilities that weren't limited by reality.

The characters were relatable and understandable; their struggles were something I could relate to as they grappled with love, career choices and making decisions that felt right. And even though nothing ever comes easy in life, romance books made it seem like anything was possible. Like there was an infinite amount of paths leading to success. It was comforting knowing that even when times got tough, I could pick up a book and escape to another world where things eventually worked out for the best.

One afternoon, as I flipped through a women's magazine, I stumbled upon a self-test titled "What Relationship Do You Have?" Curiosity piqued, I decided to give it a go. The test comprised ten questions. I took a deep breath and decided to play the game and let the magazine gods tell me whether I'm compatible with Tim.

How often do you and your partner communicate openly about your feelings and concerns?

Openly? Well, we don't talk at all right now...

Are you both able to compromise and find solutions during conflicts?

I guess taking the time apart to contemplate was considered a solution to a conflict? At least partially...

Do you feel supported and encouraged by your partner in pursuing your goals and dreams?

I didn't like where it was going...

Are there shared interests and activities that you both enjoy?

I guess I could take up jogging.

How often do you and your partner spend quality time together?

I just said I could take up jogging.

Do you feel respected and valued in your relationship?

It's not that Tim doesn't respect me. He just doesn't have time to do it properly, seeing as he's always away.

Are you satisfied with the level of intimacy and emotional connection in your partnership?

Why am I thinking of Nico here? We're not in a partnership. Tim and I are.

Are there trust and mutual respect between you and your partner?

I feel like I have answered this question already?

How well do you handle disagreements?

Not very well...

Do you have shared goals and a vision for the future as a couple?

We did in the beginning. Time to revisit that, I guess.

I had a feeling that I would not like the outcome of the test. I summarized the points and checked the result on the next page: "There is hope to make it better."

Great. The hope dies last. I chuckled to myself, feeling a little silly for seeking advice in a magazine test. Yet, deep down, I couldn't ignore the possibility of it being true. Perhaps there was indeed hope for Tim and me, a chance to rebuild what was broken.

Contemplating my almost failing relationship and our future, thoughts of Nico resurfaced. It had been a while since his confession about not being able to stop thinking about me. I wondered what he was doing, whether he had reunited with that woman and whether he was happy. Curiosity gnawed at me, and a thought crossed my mind—maybe they should take the magazine test and see where their path led them.

Just as I was scrutinizing my relationship, Natalia burst through the door, her eyes shining with excitement. "Erica, guess what? Roman is taking me for a trip to Luxemburg!" she exclaimed, unable to contain her joy.

I smiled, genuinely happy for her. "That's fantastic, Natalia! I'm thrilled for you!" I gave her a hug. She was flushed and excited.

Natalia settled onto the couch, eager to share. "I hope Roman would finally be the man I would settle with. I really like him and he seems like a man my family could approve of.

I sense Natalia yearned to show her relatives that life abroad could be enriching and bring good things into life.

Her words resonated within me, stirring a yearning of my own. Natalia's boldness reminded me that life was meant to be lived to the fullest, that we shouldn't confine ourselves to the familiar. As I pondered her journey, an idea began to form—an idea that maybe, just maybe, there was a happy ending for me, too.

With Natalia away on her trip, I found myself with a few days alone in her apartment. Out of sheer boredom, I turned to YouTube for entertainment, stumbling upon salsa dance videos. Intrigued, I started watching and, to my surprise, found myself captivated by the rhythmic movements and passionate energy.

Wine and chocolate became my companions on that particular evening. In my state of relaxation, I made a decision—it was time to talk to Tim. I wanted to share my thoughts and desires. I wanted to express my longing for a relationship filled with open communication, growth, and a shared vision for the future. There was hope, after all. The magazine said it.

After days of deliberation and soul-searching, I was ready to confront Tim. Time to have an honest conversation about our relationship. I texted him, arranging a meeting at our apartment. Tim replied, almost instantly eager to see me. It was a make-or-break moment, and I was ready to lay it all on the line.

As I stepped into the familiar space of our apartment, a mix of nervousness and determination coursed through my veins. Tim was already there, waiting for me in the living room. His eyes met mine, searching for answers, and I could sense a hint of concern in his gaze.

"Hey, Erica. I'm glad you wanted to talk," Tim said, his voice laced with apprehension.

I took a deep breath, mustering the courage to speak my truth. "Tim, we need to have a tough conversation. There are some things I need to express, things I expect from our relationship moving forward."

He nodded, his expression a blend of curiosity and apprehension. "I understand. Go ahead. I'm ready to listen."

I walked closer to him, my heart pounding in my chest. It was time to lay everything bare, to speak from the depths of my desires. To speak about the boundaries I needed in our relationship.

"Tim, I want us to have open and honest communication." I spoke with a mixture of vulnerability and determination. "We've been avoiding important discussions and sweeping things under the rug for too long. I need to feel like my voice is being heard, and I want you to be able to express your feelings as well. Let's address our fears, our dreams, and our insecurities without holding back. Can you commit to that?"

I felt like I said too much. Would he understand me? Was it possible that a man could actually give all this to me? I wouldn't know.

He looked at me intently, his gaze searching. "Erica, I hear you. And I want the same. I want us to be able to have those conversations without fear or resentment. I know I haven't been the best at communicating, but I'm willing to learn and grow alongside you."

Wow. He did hear me. His words sparked a flicker of hope within me. Maybe, just maybe, we could salvage what we once had. As I considered the path forward, Tim surprised me with an unexpected revelation.

"In fact, Erica, I have something to share with you," Tim said, a glimmer of excitement in his eyes. "I've been doing some thinking as well, and I've taken a step towards a fresh start. I've rented another apartment, a bigger and nicer one. I thought we could move there together and leave this place as an Airbnb for now."

He surprised me. Tim, who doesn't do anything rash. A guy I thought was stuck in his old ways did something spontaneous. I wasn't sure how I'd felt about it. I was taken aback by his revelation, my mind racing to process the implications. A new apartment meant a new beginning, a chance to create a space that was truly ours. It was a bold move, one that signaled Tim's commitment to change and growth. It was also creating distance between me and Nico. A distance that could help to start fresh with my boyfriend.

"That's...surprising, Tim," I stammered, a mix of astonishment and intrigue flooding my thoughts. "I didn't expect this. Are you sure about it?"

He nodded, a determined smile gracing his lips. "I am. I want us to start fresh, to build something better together. This new apartment represents that for me. Will you give it a chance, Erica? Will you give us a chance?"

As I contemplated his words, I couldn't deny the flicker of hope that burned within me. There was something familiar in Tim's eyes, a glimmer of the person I fell in love with. Could this fresh start be the key to rekindling what we had lost?

Chapter 18

In the days that followed, the process of moving out began, transforming our once-shared space into a maze of cardboard boxes and half-empty rooms. As I navigated the staircase, struggling to maintain my balance with an armful of belongings, fate intervened, intertwining my path with Nico's once again.

I bumped into him, our unexpected collision breaking the trance of my thoughts. Nico's surprise mirrored my own, his eyes widening as he took in the scene of me amidst the chaos of the move. The air crackled with unspoken words, a silent acknowledgment of the emotions that had consumed us both.

"Nico," I said his name, my voice filled with a mixture of warmth and regret.

His lips curled into a small, bittersweet smile. "Erica, it's been quite a while." He looked at the boxes in my hands. "Are you moving out?"

Before I could answer, Tim appeared by my side, his attention consumed by the logistics of the move.

"Hey, Nico," Tim said, his voice tinged with distracted energy. "Good to see you. We're just getting everything ready for the move. Exciting times!"

His enthusiastic greeting to Nico was brief, a mere veneer of neighborly courtesy overshadowed by the pressing task at hand.

Nico nodded. He scratched his neck and shifted his body. "I didn't realize things are going so well between you and Tim." he said in a lower voice. It wasn't a question, merely a fact, he stated.

My stomach was twisting. I wanted to talk to Nico properly, without Tim running around and without boxes in my hand. I wanted to tell him so much, but the thought of the woman picking up his phone stopped me. If I continue this two men's attraction, I'll end up with nothing.

I smiled at Nico and tried to walk away, boxes getting heavier in my arms. He gently grabbed my elbow to stop me. I hoped Tim wouldn't see us.

"Erica, I've been thinking a lot about everything that happened between us," Nico began, his voice laced with a mixture of regret and longing. "I can't help but wonder if we made the right choices, if we let something special slip away."

Oh no. My mind was racing. Nico, not now. Not when I made the decision to be with Tim. I needed to be strong and stick to the plan.

"I don't know, Nico," I said, my voice steady but tinged with a touch of vulnerability. "We had our moments. But sometimes, we have to accept that certain paths are not meant to be traveled together."

Nico looked into my eyes. He was searching for hope in my determination. I needed to stay strong. The attraction I felt to this man was overwhelming, but I made my choice.

Finally, Nico nodded, his gaze shifting to the chaotic scene unfolding around us. "You're right. Life has a funny way of leading us down unexpected roads. I just... I hope you find the happiness you deserve, Erica."

"I hope the same for you, Nico," I responded, my voice filled with a mixture of gratitude and nostalgia. "We may have taken different paths, but I believe that both of us have the potential to find happiness and fulfillment."

Nico nodded in acknowledgment, his gaze lingering on me for a moment longer than necessary. I could sense his desire to argue his case further. But the timing was not on our side, and with a silent nod, he turned towards the stairs.

Why was this so painful?

Carrying the weight of boxes and the weight of my own indecision, I continued the arduous task of packing our memories into the van. With each step, doubts gnawed at the corners of my mind, questioning the road I was about to embark upon. Was I making the right decision by giving Tim another chance? Could we truly rebuild what was broken and find happiness once more?

As the day wore on, the once-familiar walls of our apartment grew emptier, echoing with the ghosts of our shared past. There was something undeniably comforting in the familiarity of Tim, in the shared memories and history we held. And yet, the lingering presence of Nico reminded me of the depth of emotions left unexplored, the path not taken.

With cautious optimism, I resolved to take a leap of faith. I would give our relationship another shot, knowing that the path ahead would be riddled with challenges and uncertainties. Love, after all, was not without its share of complexities and struggles. Perhaps it was in the face of adversity that we discovered our true strength and the depth of our love.

As we closed the doors of our old apartment for the last time, I looked ahead to the future. The possibilities that awaited us in our new home promised a fresh start and the potential for renewal. The journey wouldn't be easy, and doubts would continue to tug at the corners of my heart. But perhaps, just perhaps, this shared endeavor would lead us to a place of renewed love and happiness—a place where our souls could intertwine once again in a harmonious rhythm.

Our new apartment, nestled in a modern part of Zurich, was a breath of fresh air. With its sleek design and contemporary aesthetic, it exuded a sense of sophistication and new beginnings. The moment I stepped inside, I felt a wave of excitement and anticipation wash over me. This was our chance for a fresh start, a chapter filled with possibilities.

As I admired the clean lines and minimalist decor, a mix of emotions stirred within me. The anticipation of starting anew with Tim, combined with the lingering doubts from our past, created an inner conflict that tugged at my heart. I yearned for a relationship built on trust, respect, and love, but I couldn't ignore the toxic patterns that had haunted us before.

Exploring the neighborhood, I noticed it was filled with families and their pets. The sight of children playing and dogs wagging their tails brought a smile to my face, and yet a pang of uncertainty tugged at the corners of my mind. Would this be the environment where Tim could finally leave his toxic behavior behind? Was he truly ready to build something meaningful together?

The walls of our new apartment, with their clean slate, mirrored the fresh start we were striving for. They whispered promises of a love that could conquer our past mistakes and redefine our relationship. Each day, as we settled into our new home, I observed Tim's actions, searching for signs of growth and change. The moments of tenderness and affection warmed my heart, offering glimmers of hope that perhaps we could build something beautiful together.

With each passing day, as we navigated the challenges and celebrated the small victories, I allowed myself to believe in the power of our new beginning. Our apartment became a symbol of hope and resilience, a reminder that we were not defined by our past but by the choices we made in the present. The lingering thoughts of Nico kept lurking in my mind, but I was waving them away. There was no point in thinking about him and what could have been. Even if I'd change my mind now, it was too late. I told him to go and be happy and forget me. He probably did this by now, anyway. There it was a pang in my heart at the thought of him being with another woman. But why should I deny him happiness when I was clearly fighting for mine?

Chapter 19

As the days turned into weeks in our new apartment, the space began to take on a sense of familiarity and comfort. The modern design and the abundance of natural light breathed life into the rooms, creating an atmosphere of serenity. It was as if I finally had some room to breathe, some space for myself. Tim and I were slowly settling into our new life together, embracing the fresh start.

Amidst the busyness of unpacking and organizing, I still found time to meet Natalia often. I needed to know what was happening in the outside world. I took a week off to organize everything in the new place. Natalia kept me up to date on gossip and work news. The full-blown summer only added to the allure of our meetings. We often found ourselves spending late afternoons by the lake, basking in the sun's warmth and having cocktails. It kept us happy and relaxed.

“I have to admit,” Natalia said one afternoon. “I never expected Tim to really come through.”

Tim’s work situation had shifted, allowing him to spend more evenings at home. It was a welcome change, as it meant that we could see each other more frequently and have meaningful conversations about our day. I cherished these moments, relishing in the connection we were building and the hope of a future filled with love and understanding.

“I’m so glad he did!” Natalia added. “I was so close to having a little talk with him myself!”

“That would surely go well,” I snorted.

Natalia’s direct way of communicating could have been too much to Tim. He preferred either not to talk about things or be as diplomatic as possible. Only with me. He felt comfortable enough to voice his concerns. Not in a way I enjoyed most of the time. The last weeks, however, showed so much improvement that I hoped those days were over and we could talk with love and respect.

Going back to work was quite painful. Coming back after a week off to the hundreds of emails and work colleagues wanting to discuss things, a deadline for a major project at work loomed closer. My schedule grew increasingly hectic. The demands of my job consumed my time and energy, leaving little room for leisure or relaxation.

Despite my busy schedule, I made a conscious effort to share more of my life with Tim. I would recount stories of Natalia's dating escapades and the colorful characters we encountered along the way.

One evening, as we sat side by side at home with our laptops. I was diligently finishing some last-minute emails and Tim was engrossed in his own work. A sense of tension hung in the air. My heart sunk. I recognized this mood of his. Something was not right. Tim's brows were furred, and he kept banging his fingers on the keyboard, giving me a look from time to time.

I closed my laptop and turned to face him, searching his eyes for answers. "Tim," I started cautiously, "Is there something bothering you? You seem a bit off today."

He sighed heavily, his gaze wavering. "It's just that... I think you should consider changing jobs. Your work consumes too much of your time, and because of that, we don't have enough time for ourselves."

My heart dropped at his words, and anger surged within me. How can he make such accusations when he was the one working late every night, ignoring my existence? Where did this suddenly come from?

Struggling to keep my voice even, I said, "Changing jobs isn't really an option right now. I like what I do and am managing despite the workload."

He shifted uneasily in his seat before continuing, "It's not just about your job, though. It's also about you spending so much time with Natalia. She is your friend, but I can't help but think her influence might be affecting our relationship."

Anger coursed through me, and my hands shook with frustration. "Tim, you can't just make assumptions like that. Natalia has nothing to do with us—you need to trust me and stop trying to control whom I talk to."

Then something passed over his face, and he stammered out a response. "Well, I thought maybe you wanted to start a family eventually and Natalia seems like the kind of girl who may keep us from having one..."

My breath caught in my throat, and anger surged inside me. Had we not just come through a crisis together? And now he was telling me to abandon my dearest friend and start a family with him? It made no sense.

"You mean... having a baby now?" I asked, my voice filled with disbelief. Tim refused to look at me.

The room grew quiet as tensions rose; the influx of insecurity was palpable. It was our first major disagreement in our new apartment—a clash of expectations and anxieties that had been festering for too long. And yet, I stood my ground, unwilling to give in to his ridiculous demands.

"You ask me to change job and abandon my friend as if it would fix our problems? We did a good progress I think but we are nowhere near to figuring this out. The demands you make today are an example of that. You've never even proposed to me, and now you're talking about having kids? We need to figure out what's wrong with us first, patch up the holes in our relationship, and nurture our love before we can think of making such big decisions."

As I was talking, Tim's face softened. "You're right, Erica. I didn't realize how strongly you felt about this. Let's take a step back and focus on building a stronger foundation. I want us to be better together."

A sense of relief washed over me. He understood. Without any further comments. Without more criticism, he actually admitted I'm right. I wasn't ready to become a mother—not now, not while our relationship was in such a fragile state.

Tim pulled me closer and wrapped his arms around me. "I love you, Erica."

And that's when my stomach would tie into a knot and I would get a weird feeling. Was I trying to explain everything rationally? Or was I too stubborn and too proud to see that my feelings for Tim were dying in a speed of light? The fight between my head—the rational one, and my heart—full of feelings and desires. I kept having a picture of Nico on the staircase, telling me we might be making a mistake.

As if he sensed me from afar, my phone vibrated and a push notification showed a familiar name. I saw Tim glancing at my phone curiously.

The screen went off again, and I pretended to not be bothered by the message that arrived. The curiosity was burning me from the inside, but I didn't want to risk Tim getting suspicious. I got up and left my laptop and my phone on the sofa next to Tim.

"Would you like some coffee?" I asked.

Tim shook his head. "It's way too late for a coffee. You shouldn't have any either or you'll be awake till early morning."

I rolled my eyes. We were both adults. I didn't need him to tell me what I should or shouldn't. I guess I couldn't expect all his habits to improve. I tried to be nice and got another lecture. I had a feeling that Tim was the one who had no idea how to be in a relationship—not me.

I walked into the kitchen and made an espresso just to spite Tim. I was planning to drink it in front of him to make my point. I wasn't perfect either. When something triggered me, it was hard to play nice.

Walking back in, my heart skipped a beat. Tim was holding my phone, frowning.

"Tim, what the—"

"Why is your salsa teacher texting you this late?" He looked at me, demanding answers.

I calculated in my head how much he could have found out from the preview snippet. He did not have my PIN and so he could only read the first line of the message. He had no idea it was Nico texting, nor would he connect the dots that Nico was our neighbor in the old apartment.

"Well?" Tim stood up, looking expectant.

"Give me my phone and I can tell you," I said, trying to keep my voice steady.

"I'd like an answer first," Tim said, anger burning his eyes.

I knew that I had deleted all texts we ever exchanged with Nico. Which means there was a chance to get out of this. As long as Nico didn't write something obvious. I guessed he probably didn't, otherwise Tim would be much angrier now.

"How can I know why a teacher is texting me when I didn't see the damn text, Tim?" I held my hand out for my phone. "I can show it to you afterwards," I added. I really hoped I wouldn't regret that promise.

Tim handed over my phone and stood very close, waiting.

The message was brief:

Hey, I hope you're doing well in your new apartment. I noticed you stopped coming to salsa. Please do not resign on my account.

I took a deep breath. Okay, I can work with that. It wasn't that bad.

"There you go. Read it." I said and pushed my phone in his hand, making sure he noticed my frustration.

Tim scanned the message quickly. "Why do you tell some teacher about moving apartments? And why didn't you tell me you quit salsa?" The second part made him visibly happy.

"I didn't want you to, yet again, comment on my hobbies. So I didn't mention it." That was actually true. I didn't want Tim to say 'I told you so'. After all, he had no idea what the reason was.

"Why does this person say you might have quit on their account?" Tim looked suspicious. "Were they giving you trouble?"

I hated this conversation. Trying to think of ways to get out of it, I did the best I could to give an explanation that would make sense to Tim. "The teacher was impatient and I was a little annoyed at that. I told the school that I am quitting because I moved and the travel would be inconvenient. But the teacher might have noticed it was his fault. Anyway, I tried to make no big deal out of it, so please just give me the phone back and let this go."

Tim was considering it for a moment. My explanation seemed to make sense to him. I was fuming inside at having to lie. Angry at Tim for trying to invade my privacy. Annoyed at Nico for complicating my life again. But most of all, I was angry at myself for having my feelings split between the two men. For convincing myself that there was a way to repair things with Tim. For moving to another apartment when, deep down, I knew I should have let Tim move alone.

I didn't know if I was acting out or because my heart finally got a say in all this. The words I was afraid of finally left my lips.

"Tim, we're done. I can't do this anymore."

Chapter 20

"Erica, you can't be serious—"

"We're done, Tim. I shouldn't have moved here with you. I should have given up much earlier and save us both all the hustle. I cannot continue like that. I can't even drink a damn espresso whenever I want!"

"I only want what's the best for you!" he said without looking at me. His face was pale, and he hid his hands in the pockets of his jeans.

"Shouldn't I know what's the best for me?"

"Erica, let's talk about this. We were doing much better. Why not give it a chance?" Tim was pleading.

I sighed. "Tim, I am out of chances. For you, for us, for myself. I need to figure out things in my life. What I know is that we don't have a future together."

"I can't believe you're doing this," Tim's voice changed now. It was trembling and his face was getting red. "After all, I did for you! I helped you move here, helped you get a job and live in a great country. I was working overtime so we could manage—"

I couldn't believe how different his reality was from mine. How far away from each other we were! "Tim, you didn't help me get the job. I did it on my own. I got a visa to work here. As for your working overtime, you always claimed you're trying to make something out of yourself."

At this point, I wondered what the point was discussing anything with this man. I couldn't recognize him. It was time to move on. I was happy that not all of my things were unpacked yet.

"I would like to stay at your old apartment seeing as we don't have more bookings at the moment," I said. Tim opened his mouth, but I was faster. "I will pay you, of course. So you don't feel like I am using you."

"You're serious." Tim whispered. He finally realized that I meant what I was saying. That this time it was over.

"I am. And I would love if we could do split in peace. We tried, and it didn't work out. It might be a shock to your right now but think about the times where you felt disappointed in me. When we fought about silly things and how different our lifestyle is."

Tim dropped to the sofa, covering his face with his hands. I stood there in front of him, wanting to disappear. He was hurting. But so was I.

"Don't you want to sleep on it?" Tim asked. "It's late now. You can go in the morning. I can sleep on the sofa," he offered.

I wanted to leave. The atmosphere was so heavy it was suffocating.

The next hour seemed like five minutes. I grabbed the essentials, called the taxi, and was now standing in the middle of an empty apartment. I told Tim I'd get my things in the coming days. He didn't stop me. The resignation was visible on his face. On the one hand, I felt bad about doing this to him. On the other, there was such a relief in my heart. It wasn't the first time I broke up with someone. This time, however, our relationship had gotten beyond what I normally went through. Other men were just flings while Tim was going to be a partner for life...

The apartment looked different from what it was before. The furniture was simple and clearly to cater for short-stay guests.

"I really need to find my own apartment," I said out loud to myself.

It was not ideal to be in a place full of memories. Even without Tim, it all felt like I was still stuck. And the uncomfortable proximity of Nico did not help my anxiety. I wasn't feeling like running into him and explaining why

I'm back. I wanted to close all the open chapters and focus on starting anew. Getting a new apartment to live in, in a neighborhood far away from Tim and Nico, seemed like a right solution.

It was time to get myself together. Let's see it as a new adventure. From now on, I was free to do as I please!

Chapter 21

Hunting apartments in Zurich is absolutely crazy. Here I am, a newly single thirty-four-year-old woman trying to get an apartment by myself. When you go to the viewing, it's either forty people queue all applying for the same place or the apartment is only rented for a limited amount of time. You are judged the moment you say hello to the person showing you around. It will be either the owner or the current tenant, both scanning you from top to bottom, displeased with your lack of German and judging your marital status. I've heard people at work telling me I need to be extra nice, try to get on their good side, make sure they remember me and overall emit the perfect tenant vibe. It was exhausting!

Last week, an elegant older lady was showing me around.

"I live in the penthouse upstairs, you know?" she pointed her finger to the ceiling.

"I see," I replied.

"I might be old, but I'm not deaf," she said, determination in her eyes. "I hear everything!"

"Ok." I started getting uncomfortable.

"You're single, right?" She asked, her hands propped on her hips.

"Ye—"

"Well, I shall have no men in this building! If you want the apartment, I can consider you, but there shall be no men!" she was pointing the finger at me now.

I decided to never apply for that apartment. 'No men' rule didn't even scare me at the moment. After the latest events, I wouldn't mind just having a bit of a breather before going back to dating. But, oh boy, the lady was scary. I wondered if she was ever married or whether she scared away all available candidates!

If only the apartment I was staying in didn't belong to my ex. But the search must continue.

Another day, I stood in front of yet another apartment.

"Miss Davis?" a man in his fifties opened the door.

"That's right, hello!" I shook the man's hand a bit too enthusiastically. He didn't wince, but grinned at me instead. That was a good start.

"Please come in." He motioned for me to enter. The apartment seemed lovely. Bright, lively and spotless.

"So the price is as stated in the ad, right?" I asked, surprised how cheap it seemed for the apartment this big.

"That's correct." he nodded.

We walked around, looking at each of the rooms. The man opened the last door. "Here would be your bedroom."

I stopped in my tracks. "What do you mean? Am I not allowed to choose where I sleep?"

The man shook his head. "The other bedroom is mine."

Whoa.

"Umm- what do you mean yours? I thought this apartment will be vacant soon?"

He laughed. "Oh no, no. I am looking for a flat-mate. That's how you call it in English, right?" He grinned at me again. "I think you would be perfect!" This time, his smile was a kind of creepy.

Perfect flat-mate. How did he assess that? Just by looking at me? I had to get out of here.

"Thank you so much for your kind offer," I said, walking fast to the exit. "I will keep in touch!"

The man looked confused and tried to call out, but I was already out the front door.

That's what it boils down to, Erica. Either you live in your ex's apartment next door to a man you fancy or you would become a flat-mate of a creepy older guy to watch you walk around in your pajamas. Oh, the choices were so alluring!

·♥·♥·♥·♥·♥·

Natalia burst into laughter after hearing my stories of the apartment hunting. She knew exactly how difficult it was to find one as a foreigner. She was lucky enough to have her uncle help her in that regard.

"Doesn't your uncle know of any other free place?" I asked hopefully.

"I'll be sure to ask him," she promised. "Any more viewings planned?"

I looked at my notes. So old-fashioned with my paper notebook instead of the phone. Millennials were funny this way. Some things we loved doing digitally, and some had to be analogue.

"Just one more, close to Bellevue. A studio."

"Oh, that's a nice area!"

"Yeah, that's why I'm not sure I should even go. There will be a hundred people wanting it."

"I can come with you and decide there. We could go to Tibits afterwards and have a nice meal," Natalia offered.

"That sounds wonderful, but don't you have salsa tonight?" I asked as I realized it was Friday. I completely lost track of time and only sometimes resurfaced to realize yet another week went by.

"The first-level course finished already and the second one starts only in two weeks."

I nodded, thinking of how much salsa I could already dance if it weren't for everything crashing down in my life.

"Nico was really down, you know," Natalia said, studying my face. "The last few times I could tell something was bothering him."

I sighed. "Well, it's not like I can reach out to him now. Not after all, I said to him."

"Does he even know you are back living in his building?"

I shook my head. "I am like a cat sneaking down the stairs, making sure no one hears me."

Natalia laughed out loud. She was sitting at my desk and now everyone was looking at us. I slapped her shoulder playfully. "Behave. Those people are just waiting to have something to gossip about."

Natalia stuck out her tongue and smiled. "Alright darling. Off I go pretend to do some work. Let's meet downstairs before the rush hour."

She blew me a kiss and her high heels echoed in the room. All men turning their heads to look at my gorgeous best friend.

Zurich didn't have a main square or a center per se. It was a city full of charming corners. The two places considered central were the major shopping street called Bahnhofstrasse and the Bellevue. Bahnhofstrasse was always full of rich people shopping at Chanel, Louis Vuitton, getting yet another watch at Rolex or IWC. Others just enjoyed sitting at the bars outside, close to the tram tracks, and watching people passing by. Sunday was the only day when everything was closed and the street would become a ghost town.

Bellevue, on the other hand, was a place where people enjoyed themselves sitting on the wooden benches directly at the edge of the lake. They would hang their legs down to the water to be occasionally snapped at by a swan. I sometimes saw people pouring beer down the lake. They would explain that swans need a drink and feeding them all kinds of food definitely not suitable for the birds. I rarely let my legs down, not trusting those creatures. They might have looked beautiful, but they could often be aggressive, hissing at people and pets.

I used to come here often with Natalia. We enjoyed sitting by the lake, watching people playing instruments. Sometimes we played a game, rating the men passing by. Very superficial, I know, but how entertaining! Men would flash us smiles and get more points for that.

Now, we parked Natalia's car in the underground parking lot below the opera house. We made our way to the apartment, as it was only five minutes away.

"It would be so great to live around here! It's one of the best areas in Zurich!" Natalia was excited.

I smiled and crossed my fingers, hoping I could start anew in a lively neighborhood.

The apartment was situated on the ground floor of an old tenement. It was cold inside the hall even though it was a hot summer day. We approached the old-fashioned gray door. The label said the current tenant was called *Romero*. Surprisingly, that there was no one else waiting to see the apartment.

"How strange," I said. "I expect a long queue!"

Natalia rang the doorbell. "Let's see!"

The door opened, and for a moment, I held my breath. A tall, dark-haired man with deep brown eyes stood before us.

"Hello there!" He flashed a perfect smile. "You're here for the viewing, right?"

I nodded, unable to let any word out of my mouth. For a brief moment, I thought it was Nico at the doorstep. He looked so similar! But it wasn't him, it was just my mind playing with me.

"I'm Sergio, pleased to meet you ladies!" He shook our hands and invited us in.

Natalia quickly fixed her hair when Sergio looked away. "I'm Natalia! Wonderful to meet you! This is Erica."

"Are you the one searching for an apartment, then?" Sergio asked Natalia.

"Umm, no, unfortunately not!" Natalia laughed slightly too loud.

"It's me," I said.

"Wonderful, follow me and I will show you around!" Sergio said.

I rolled my eyes at Natalia. Sergio must have made an impression on her. Usually, she dismissed men quickly, in a confident manner. When her voice pitched like the time when Roman came to salsa class, I knew she was into him.

"Get a grip!" I whispered to her. "I need this apartment!"

"You don't know who this is, do you?" she whispered back.

I looked at Sergio's back, all about him looking so familiar. But I didn't know this man.

"So we have a kitchen here and the door to the backyard," Sergio turned towards us. Natalia's explanation would have to wait till later.

"It's lovely," I said, looking around.

"In the next room, there is a bedroom with living space and a bathroom right next to it."

"It's a generous size for a studio in Bellevue," Natalia said. She was curling a strand of hair around her finger. I almost started laughing at her silliness. I wondered what happened to Roman.

"It certainly is! I probably shouldn't say this," Sergio looked at me. "- but I have expected more people to be interested. So far, it was just you."

"Really?" I was hoping this was my chance.

"Yes! That's unusual. With other properties that belong to my family, we usually do not even have a viewing like this. It is all done by our agents."

"Is there something wrong with it?" I laughed and then blushed because I realized I said it out loud.

Luckily, Sergio found it amusing. "No, it's perfect. In fact, I have lived here for almost a year and I promise you it's in a great shape!"

Natalia murmured under her breath. "It's you who's in perfect shape." I tried to control myself, but it was hard not to burst into laughter.

"I would imagine you living in a villa rather than in a small apartment like that," Natalia said. She was looking at me, trying to give me a hint.

Sergio gave Natalia a wink. "Well, me and my brothers like to have a place of solitude. It's hectic enough to be a Romero the whole day long. Coming back to a place that's so normal definitely helps to relax."

I finally realized. This place belonged to Sergio Romero. Of the Romeros family! The Colombian tycoons that made fortune in Switzerland.

"I'm so sorry! I only have realized now. I have seen you on tv! I haven't been living in Switzerland long!" I blushed, trying to explain to a millionaire why I didn't know who he was. It was too much information already. He didn't care about my life. Better act like a sane person.

Sergio grinned. "No worries! So would you like to apply for the apartment? Seeing as you're the first one, I am happy to approve your application."

"Heck, yeah!" I cried.

Chapter 22

I was over the moon. Just like Sergio promised, they have approved my application. I was to move in to my very own apartment in two weeks' time. I couldn't believe my luck. Not only was this a perfect little place in a wonderful location, my landlord was a celebrity. Sergio even left his private phone number in case I needed anything. It was as if the universe was helping me to set on a new adventure. One where I put myself in the first place and don't try to be someone I am not just to be loved.

I still had to face Tim to get all my stuff. I couldn't believe I was so naive to move with him to the new apartment. You cannot change a man like Tim, so set in his ways and convinced whatever he does is how it should be done. I was sure he would try to make me stay, so I asked Natalia to accompany me this time.

Tim wasn't home when we arrived, nor did he pick up the phone. It was very unlike him. I felt strange, like something wasn't right.

"Tim's fine. He finally realized it is time to set you free," Natalia said, packing my things in the boxes. She moved around energetically, as if wanting to get me out of here as fast as possible. I was impressed by how she managed to carry boxes out the door in high heels and not lose balance in the slightest.

Maybe she was right. Tim finally gave up, and I only felt weird because it was so easy this time. No toxic behavior, no promises he couldn't keep, no playing victim. He just gave me space to end this chapter. I should be thankful. We had our closure multiple times already.

I took a day off to get keys to my new apartment. HR wouldn't give me more than that, seeing as I just moved to another place. I didn't want to tell them what kind of failure I was changing flats so many times because my relationship was a disaster. I had Natalia to help. She was determined to meet Sergio again and wouldn't miss the key handover.

"Whatever happened to Roman?" I asked. She hasn't been talking about him for a while now.

Natalia shrugged. “I didn’t want to tell you. I feel so embarrassed.”

“Natalia, come on. It’s me! You can tell me anything.”

Natalia sighed. Her attitude instantly changed from cheerful to sad. “I discovered Roman had a wife and children.”

I gasped. How did I miss that? I felt so bad neglecting my best friend. It must have felt awful.

“That’s terrible! Why didn’t you tell me sooner?”

“You had so much going on—“

“I always want to know what’s going on with you!” I grabbed her hands. “You’re my rock, Natalia! And I want to be yours! You’re a wonderful friend, and I am so thankful to have you in my life.”

“I’m so happy we’ve met,” Natalia smiled.

“Please remember, you can always rely on me. Sorry I was so invested in my own problems I haven’t noticed yours!”

Natalia waved her hand. “Don’t worry about that. My grandma always said there’s more where it came from.”

I was impressed by how strong she was. And yet I was worried that she might be putting a wall around her. That after situations like that, she might let no one in.

“There will be someone for you and me. You’ll see. We will manifest them.” I grinned.

“Why don’t we manifest them tonight after we’re done at your new place?”

I knew exactly what she suggested. “I guess it’s party night?”

She nodded. “I wish we could party with the handsome Sergio.”

“Why don’t you manifest it?” I grinned.

But our manifesting powers must have been on holidays. Not only would Sergio join us tonight, he didn’t even show up for the key handover. Instead, the Romero family agent arrived with all the paperwork. I signed my first ever rent contract in Switzerland and felt like I finally had my life under control.

Chapter 23

The moment the agent left the apartment, Natalia couldn't contain her excitement. She immediately popped open the first bottle of prosecco. The cork rocketed towards the ceiling, narrowly missing my head, and the foam cascaded over the polished wooden floor, creating a sticky mess.

It wasn't the greatest start to being a well-behaved tenant, but we couldn't help ourselves. We burst into laughter; the sound echoing through the walls. In that carefree moment, we felt like mischievous teenagers, unburdened by the weight of the world. We danced around the small apartment. Latin music was filling the air as we swirled and jumped, letting the rhythm get rid of the residual negativity from our hearts.

With each dance step, our worries and heartaches seemed to dissipate, replaced by a renewed sense of hope and optimism. The spilled prosecco on the floor became a testament to our carefree spirits. It was a reminder that sometimes it's okay to let go and embrace the messy moments of life. It's not like Tim would walk in and give me a disappointing look for simply being happy.

In that moment, as Natalia and I stood breathless and grinning at each other, I made a silent vow to myself. I wouldn't allow anyone to diminish the importance of the friendships that had shaped me and brought me peace. True happiness, I realized, could only thrive in an environment of trust, acceptance, and mutual understanding.

"Let's dress up!" Natalia giggled and ran to the bedroom, almost slipping on the prosecco puddle.

I realized I am drunker than I thought. The first drinks always went straight to my head.

Natalia came back with a shopping bag and threw it on the floor in front of me. I looked suspiciously at the bag, wondering what Natalia was up to.

"Come on, open it!" She encouraged me.

In the bag, there were two wigs, one luminescent pink and another blue. Natalia grabbed a pink bob, and I was left with a blue Rapunzel-like one. I tried to keep a straight face, but I couldn't stop giggling. Natalia already put hers on. She looked fun and sexy, which I'm sure I will not be when I put my wig on.

"I thought we're going out?" I asked, holding the wig in my hand.

"We still can go later!" Natalia pulled two colorful feather boas out of the bag.

"Jeez, what kind of celebration is this?" I was crying now.

"It's a house-warming party! Just roll with it, girl!" Natalia sang in her Eastern accent.

I put my wig on, wrapped the boa around my neck and finished strong with a bright pink lipstick. I heard a pop from the kitchen and yet another bottle spilled all over. I heard her swearing in her language.

I couldn't help but burst into laughter at the chaos unfolding around us. Natalia's infectious energy was contagious, and I couldn't resist getting swept up in the moment's madness. The sight of us, dressed in outrageous wigs and draped in colorful feather boas, was nothing short of ridiculous.

Amidst the laughter and spilled prosecco, Natalia retrieved another bottle from the kitchen and handed it to me with a mischievous grin. "Let's make this a night to remember!" she exclaimed, raising her glass.

We clinked our glasses together; the sound reverberating through the apartment. I felt a sense of liberation. It was a reminder that sometimes, amid life's challenges, it's important to let go, have fun, and embrace the unexpected.

The wigs bobbed on our heads, and the feather boas trailed behind us like vibrant trails of happiness. It didn't matter that we were making a mess, or that we were behaving like wild party animals in the confines of our own home. At that moment, we were free from judgment and inhibition.

As the night drew to a close, we collapsed onto the couch, exhausted but content. The apartment bore witness to the uninhibited celebration of life and friendship.

In that moment, as I looked at Natalia, her pink wig askew and a wide smile on her face, I felt an overwhelming sense of gratitude. Gratitude for the wild, unpredictable journey that had led us here, to this cozy apartment filled with laughter. Gratitude for the strength that came from embracing our true selves and the friendships that sustained us through life's ups and downs.

While I was pondering on life, Natalia was more practical and she was dialing the pizza place for much needed carbs.

"YEES? HE-LLO? Can we order two large Vegetarian Paradise?" Natalia was shouting on the phone. The person on the other side was either amused or annoyed. I couldn't tell. "Yes, as soon as possible! Deliver to Erica Davis! ERICA DAVIS!"

Natalia turned to me, confused. "He doesn't know where you live." She handed me the phone, and giggling, I gave the pizza man my address. He definitely wasn't amused. I added two cans of Coke and before I could say thank you, he hanged up. I couldn't blame him. We were a mess, only funny to ourselves.

As we were relaxing and slowly sobering up, the sound of the doorbell echoed through the apartment. I got up and opened the door, trying to maintain a composed demeanor despite the colorful wig still perched atop my head.

Instead of a delivery man, standing on the other side of the door was Nico. The charismatic salsa teacher who had recently entered my life and stirred up a whirlwind of emotions within me.

"Hello?" Nico looked confused. He clearly didn't recognize me.

I froze in place. It can't be happening to me again. I didn't get a chance to take a look in the mirror, but I was sure I looked like I came back from a night at the tacky costume party.

Nico stared at me, expecting any response.

"BRING ON THE PIZZA!" Natalia roared from the bedroom.

"Is Sergio here?" Nico asked, his brows furrowed.

I couldn't believe he knew Sergio! Small world, I guess, but I tried to play it to my advantage. He doesn't know it's me. I can try to send him away.

"Sergio moved out. I am the new tenant." I tried to make my voice sound different. I was so bad at acting, but I gave my best shot.

"ERICA! Where are you? I'm starving!" Natalia danced into the hallway.

My heart stopped. I couldn't look at Nico.

"Erica?" Nico asked. I looked up and saw a bewildered look in his eyes. "What on earth are you doing—here?"

"It's Nico!" Natalia stated, a little too loud.

I was so embarrassed. My face felt hot, and I didn't know how to handle this situation. I was hoping Natalia will regain some common sense quickly and come to my rescue.

Instead, Nico's laughter roared in the hall. I realized how crazy it all must have looked to him. I couldn't help but laugh.

"I still need some kind of explanation!" he said, holding his stomach.

I cleared my throat. "Well—I kind of live here now." I turned around to see where Natalia was, but she had already sneaked out of the hall to give us some space.

"Really?" Nico raised his eyebrows. "But—I thought you were moving with your boyfriend? Is he here as well?" His body tensed as if expecting a confrontation with Tim.

"He isn't," I said. "We didn't work out."

"Oh, I'm sorry to hear."

I felt a slight pang in my heart. I guess I couldn't expect him to suddenly jump out of happiness that I am newly single. I told him after all that we don't have a future together. And now he is most likely claimed by that other woman.

"Would you like to come in?" I offered. "I need a moment to look decent, but you can wait in the kitchen. I'll be right out."

"Sure." Nico walked directly towards the kitchen as if he knew exactly where it was.

I decided fixing my appearance was more important than questioning Nico. I knew I looked awful, just like the first day we've met. But looking in the mirror, I didn't realize how bad it was. What Nico saw when I opened the door was like a drunk princess who had partied all night in a drag show. Make up smeared everywhere, clothes stained with prosecco and the wig out of place.

I hurried to look like a human being again, wondering where Natalia was. I opened the bathroom door and here she was; her wig gone as well.

"I'm going to head out darling and you get your prince charming," she whispered.

"For all I know, he's not to have anymore," I whispered back.

"Don't give up," she tried to encourage me. "I'm here for you, remember?" She gave me a quick kiss on the cheek and walked towards the main door. I saw her waving to Nico, and the front door closed with a thud.

It was just me and him now.

Chapter 24

"Ah, now I recognize you," Nico smiled. "You were in my salsa class."

"Ha-ha." I envied his calm demeanor. After Natalia left, I felt very nervous.

"So you live here now?"

I nodded. "Officially from today."

"Oh, so you girls had a house-warming party! Why wasn't I invited?" He winked to show he wasn't serious.

"I think we overdid all the spilled prosecco and mess everywhere."

Nico leaned on the table and watched me. He was feeling way too comfortable in my new home. Shouldn't it be the other way round?

The doorbell rang. "It must be the pizza delivery," I said, but Nico already walked towards the door.

"Ah, Mister Nicolas!" the delivery guy greeted Nico. "I have not seen you in a while!"

How did they know each other? What was going on here? And Sergio? How was the millionaire's son involved in all this?

"Hello Omar, how is it going?" Nico replied. They were speaking English, and the man sounded foreign.

"Ah, you know, summer holidays now, so I do more deliveries! Is Mister Sergio here as well? Are you having a brother's night in?"

I froze. Did I hear them right? Brothers night in? As in Sergio and Nico? As in Nico, was one of the Romeros?

Nico finished the conversation at the door and came back with two large pizzas. He placed them on the table and looked at me. "Well, I guess the secret is out—not the way I planned on telling you."

"You mean you forgot to mention that your family is worth millions?"

"Yeah—that."

"But you lived in my building! And you're a salsa teacher!" I was confused. Was this all a charade? Was he living a double life?

"Yes, I do live in that building still. Just like Sergio lived in this apartment. It's our parents who own the villa. Me and my brothers preferred smaller places to lead a more peaceful life."

I was still in shock. I wasn't sure what bothered me more. Him not telling me he was a millionaire or the fact that he was a millionaire?

"What about salsa lessons? You don't have to earn money, do you?"

Nico chuckled. "We kind of have to earn money, but not in a way people normally do. Anyway, I teach salsa because I really like it and the salsa school belongs to me."

My eyes widened. "You're the owner?"

He nodded. "It is a good business in Zurich. People want to learn. This also brings home closer. Being surrounded by Latin music helps to miss it less," he smiled.

I understood that. I came from another continent and settled here too. It was a great place to be, but I missed Seattle often.

"So you are kind of my landlord as well, right?" I realized, blushing. The apartment was a mess, and the floor was sticky. "I promise one day you come here and I will look like a sane person and the apartment will resemble a place sane people live in!"

Nico chuckled. "I kind of like this about you."

As the realization sank in, I felt a mix of emotions swirling within me. On one hand, I was shocked by the revelation that Nico belonged to a wealthy family and had chosen to live a modest life. On the other hand, I admired his desire for simplicity and his genuine passion for salsa.

I blushed. “I still can’t believe you’re the Romero,” I said, my voice filled with a blend of surprise and curiosity. “I never would have guessed.”

“It’s no big deal, really. I can still just be your salsa teacher, if you let me—“

Nico’s eyes softened, and he reached out to take my hand, his touch both comforting and reassuring. “I didn’t want my background to define me or our connection,” he explained. “I wanted you to know me for who I am, not for the fortune my family possesses.”

Our connection. The warmth spread all over my chest.

His words resonated deep within me, reminding me of the importance of authenticity and genuine connections. It was refreshing to be in the presence of someone who valued shared experiences over material wealth.

“So, now that the secret’s out,” I began, a smile playing at the corners of my lips, “does this mean our dance lessons will come with a touch of luxury?”

Nico grinned, his eyes sparkling with mischief. “Well, perhaps I can arrange a private salsa class in a grand ballroom or a dance session overlooking the Swiss Alps.”

I laughed, feeling a weight lifted off my shoulders. Despite the initial shock, I realized that Nico’s true wealth lay not in his family’s fortune. It was in the depth of his character and the genuine connection we shared.

"Would you like to stay for a pizza?" I pointed at the table, hoping he will accept my invitation. "Or do you have to be somewhere else?"

"There's no other place I'd rather be in right now." Nico looked me straight in the eyes and I started feeling very hot in my clothes. It was as if someone turned the heating on.

As the night wore on, we devoured the pizza and engaged in playful banter. Nico had the ability to create a pleasant atmosphere where I felt myself. The apartment, once a chaotic mess, now seemed to hold an air of enchantment.

Nico and I spent the rest of the evening in each other's company, sharing stories from our lives.

He talked a lot about growing up in Colombia and moving to Switzerland as a young boy. He and his brothers grew up here with a bunch of nannies taking care of them, parents too busy building an empire. Their childhood was good, but Nico, as the youngest, often wished his mum could be more present. It was common in this country for fathers to work round the clock. But also mothers would often choose to work and hired nannies.

Once the little boys grew up to become young men, they got involved in the family affairs. Nico focused on making his dream come true and opening the dance school. He was also responsible for running the charities his family supported.

"The night you saw me in Plaza, I was meeting some investors," he explained. "Normally, I try to attend less of VIP parties and keep a low profile. It's just easier this way."

"Surely there are some good sides to being a millionaire," I chuckled. "It can't be that bad."

Nico laughed. "Of course! Don't get me wrong, I'm so proud of my parents and the way they became successful abroad. I just wanted a life where I don't attract too much attention, to live a comfortable but semi-private life."

"You managed that very well! Even Natalia didn't realize who you were," I giggled. "Sergio hasn't done this good of a job, I think."

"Sergio likes to have fun. The magazine *Blick am Abend* takes his photos occasionally."

I made a mental note to warn Natalia about Sergio's lifestyle. She was hurt enough recently.

My face expression must have changed for a moment, as Nico looked at me, his gaze filled with sincerity. "Erica, being with you feels like finding a missing piece of my heart," he confessed softly. "I may not have all the answers or the perfect plan, but I know I want to explore this connection and see where it leads us."

I decided to ignore the fact that there was another woman in his life. He surely would say something by now, wouldn't he? I smiled at Nico, my heart brimming with hope and a newfound sense of adventure. "I want that too."

Nico stood up from the sofa and extended his arms to me. I eagerly grasped his hands, feeling the electric current that pulsed between us. As he drew me closer, a captivating aroma enveloped my senses. An intoxicating blend of his carefully chosen cologne and the raw essence of his masculine musk. I trembled, knowing what will happen next.

Nico's touch was gentle yet electrifying as he caressed my cheek, his fingers sliding through my hair. With an intensity that made my heart race, he pressed his lips against mine, igniting a fire within me. The softness of his initial kiss gave way to a fierce hunger as he deepened our connection. It was a kiss that left no room for doubt or hesitation. Every nerve in my body came alive as I surrendered to the overwhelming sensation. The fluttering of butterflies in my stomach intensified, the whirlwind of emotions leaving me breathless. In that moment, time stood still, and the passion that flowed between us consumed me. Nico's arms encircled me, pulling me closer, as if he wanted to merge our souls together. The heat of his embrace matched the intensity of our kiss, and I found myself lost in a sea of desire and longing. The world around us faded into insignificance, and all that mattered was the intoxicating connection we shared.

I was lost. And found. Both at the same time. The Colombian charm overwhelmed me completely. I swear I could hear the Latin music in the background as if cheering us on.

Chapter 25

I couldn't believe the reality unfolding before me. Nico had actually kissed me, fulfilling the fantasies that had danced through my mind for weeks. The moment our lips met was nothing short of extraordinary. It was a passionate embrace that swept me off my feet, leaving me breathless and wanting more. However, the late hour and the effects of the evening's indulgence began to take their toll, overwhelming me with a sense of dizziness.

Sensing my disorientation, Nico reacted swiftly, his concern clear in his eyes. With a firm grip, he held me close, preventing me from stumbling to the floor. "Are you okay?" he asked, his voice filled with genuine worry.

Struggling to find my voice, I uttered, "Vertigo," my words barely audible. The room seemed to spin around me, and I felt the need to surrender to the fatigue that washed over me.

Against my feeble protests, Nico scooped me up in his muscular arms, effortlessly carrying me towards the bedroom. "You're going to bed," he declared, his determination unwavering.

Too tired and overwhelmed to argue, I allowed myself to be placed gently on the mattress. Nico tucked me in, covering me with the soft duvet, and planted a tender kiss on my forehead. The warmth of his touch and the soothing sound of his voice comforted me.

"Sleep well, princess," he whispered, his words a gentle lullaby. "I'm taking you on a date tomorrow night."

I groaned as I slowly opened my eyes, the throbbing headache serving as a harsh reminder of the indulgence from the previous night. Memories flooded back, the wild party, the spilled prosecco, and, most importantly, Nico's intoxicating kiss. I couldn't believe it had actually happened.

Determined to share my excitement, I reached for my phone and dialed Natalia's number. It rang a few times before she picked up.

"Hey, guess what? You won't believe what happened last night," I exclaimed, my voice filled with anticipation.

Natalia's voice came through the line, groggy but intrigued. "Nico kissed you."

"What? How do you know?"

Natalia's laughter rang through the phone. "I didn't, but I really hope you two finally get on with it! This calls for a celebration. Meet me in the city. We're going shopping!"

I quickly got ready, hoping to find the perfect dress and a stunning pair of heels to match the special evening ahead. Soon enough, Natalia and I were strolling through the bustling streets of Zurich, scouring the boutiques for the ideal ensemble.

"You need to make an impression tonight," Natalia declared, eyeing a gorgeous dress in a shop window. "Something that will leave him breathless."

I nodded in agreement, my mind filled with visions of a romantic evening. "You're right. I want to feel confident and beautiful."

As I emerged from the fitting room, Natalia's eyes widened in awe. "Erica, you look absolutely stunning!" she exclaimed, her voice filled with genuine excitement.

I twirled in front of the mirror, admiring the way the dress hugged my figure, accentuating all the right curves. The deep burgundy color complemented my complexion. The heels, with their delicate straps and stiletto heels, elevated my confidence to new heights.

Natalia clapped her hands, her enthusiasm infectious. "Nico won't know what hit him when he sees you in that dress. It's a showstopper!"

I blushed, feeling a mix of nerves and anticipation. "I hope so. I want tonight to be unforgettable."

Natalia linked her arm with mine, a mischievous glint in her eyes. "Trust me, it will be. Now, let's find some accessories to complete your look. A statement necklace, perhaps?"

We ventured further into the boutique, exploring racks of accessories and jewelry that sparkled under the store's soft lighting. Natalia's sharp eye landed on a captivating necklace, adorned with shimmering crystals in various shades of burgundy and gold.

"Erica, this is it," she declared, holding up the necklace to my neck. "It will tie your whole look together."

I nodded in agreement, the necklace instantly enhancing the elegance of the dress. As I stood there, adorned in my chosen attire, I couldn't help but feel a surge of confidence and excitement. This was the moment I had been waiting for, and I was ready to make a lasting impression on Nico.

With our shopping bags in tow, we made our way to a nearby café, settling into a cozy corner booth. As we sipped on our lattes, Natalia leaned in, her eyes brimming with curiosity.

"So, spill the details, Erica. How did it feel when he kissed you? Was it as magical as you imagined?"

A smile tugged at my lips as I reminisced about that unforgettable moment. “Natalia, it was beyond anything I could have imagined. The chemistry between us was undeniable, and his kisses... they made me feel alive, like I was floating on air.”

Natalia’s eyes sparkled with delight. “That’s what I love to hear! You two are meant to be together, Erica. I have a feeling tonight is just the beginning of something extraordinary.”

Back at my apartment, Natalia helped me prepare, fussing over my hair and makeup. “You look stunning, Erica. Now, go and have the time of your life!”

As we finished the final touches, Natalia grinned mischievously. “Well, my work here is done. I’ll disappear before your prince charming arrives. Have an amazing time, chica!”

The doorbell rang, sending a wave of nervous excitement through me. I took a deep breath and opened the door. There stood Nico, dressed impeccably in a tailored suit, a confident smile gracing his lips.

“Good evening, Erica,” he greeted me, his voice smooth and captivating. “You look absolutely breathtaking.”

Blushing, I thanked him, admiring his transformation. He had shed his previous modesty, now embracing his affluent lifestyle without reservation. Parked behind him was a sleek and luxurious car, a clear testament to his wealth.

As we made our way to the car, Nico held the door open for me, displaying an undeniable charm. I couldn't help but feel like the luckiest woman in the world.

The drive was filled with lighthearted conversation and nervous laughter. The anticipation between us was palpable. Finally, we arrived at the lakefront, where a beautiful boat awaited us. The setting sun cast a warm glow over the water, creating a picturesque scene.

Nico extended his hand, a silent invitation to step onto the boat. "Shall we, my lady?"

I took his hand, feeling a rush of excitement and anticipation. We settled on the deck, champagne glasses in hand, as we embarked on an enchanting evening.

As the boat glided across the serene lake, we watched the sun dip below the horizon, painting the sky in hues of orange and pink. Nico's gaze never left me. His eyes filled with a mixture of admiration and desire.

"You know, Erica," Nico began, his voice husky with emotion. "I never expected to meet someone like you. From the moment I saw you in my salsa class, there was something about you that captivated me."

I blushed, my heart fluttering at his words. "And I never expected to meet someone like you either, Nico. You've brought so much joy and excitement into my life."

He chuckled softly, his fingers gently intertwining with mine. "I'm glad I could be a part of your journey, Erica. Tonight has been incredible, but I want you to know that it's not just about the fancy boat or the champagne. It's about the connection we share."

I nodded, my eyes locked with his. "I feel it too, Nico. This evening has been magical, but it's the way you make me feel, the way you see me. That means the most."

He brushed his thumb against my cheek, his touch tender and filled with sincerity. "You're unlike anyone I've ever met. Your spirit, your passion, it's intoxicating. I want to explore this connection and see where it leads us."

A mixture of excitement and vulnerability washed over me, and I found myself taking a leap of faith. "I want that too, Nico. I want to explore what's between us and see where this journey takes us."

We shared a passionate kiss, sealing our unspoken commitment to each other. The night continued to unfold, filled with laughter, whispered conversations, and stolen glances that spoke volumes.

As the boat slowly made its way back to the dock, our fingers remained intertwined, unwilling to let go of the newfound connection we had discovered. The stars twinkled above us, illuminating the path ahead as we silently contemplated the possibilities that lay before us. Our lips met once again, the kiss filled with a sweet intensity that seemed to ignite a fire within us both.

Time seemed to stand still as we savored each other's company, our laughter mingling with the soft sounds of the water. It was a magical evening, filled with shared stories, stolen glances, and a growing connection that defied any expectations.

Reluctantly, the night drew to a close, and Nico drove me back to my apartment. With a sense of contentment, he walked me to my doorstep, his hand gently resting on the small of my back.

"Thank you for the most incredible evening," I whispered, my heart full.

Nico smiled, his eyes sparkling. "The pleasure was all mine, Erica. I hope this is just the beginning."

Chapter 26

As the days turned into weeks, my feelings for Nico intensified. I found myself falling deeper and deeper for him, unable to resist the magnetic pull he had on my heart. After work, we would spend our evenings together, exploring the beautiful city of Zurich and creating memories that would stay with us forever.

One evening, we decided to try out a new restaurant that had just opened in town. We sat across from each other, the candlelight casting a warm glow on our faces. Nico reached across the table, his fingers gently brushing against mine.

"You look stunning tonight," he said, his voice a soft caress.

Blushing, I thanked him and returned the compliment. We laughed and shared stories over delicious food; the time slipping away unnoticed.

After dinner, we took a leisurely stroll by the lake, hand in hand, enjoying the tranquility of the water and the beauty of the city lights reflecting on its surface. Zurich had become our playground, and every corner of the city held a special memory for us.

One day, while I was at work, I received an unexpected text message from Tim.

I hope you're doing well x

It had been a while since we broke up, and I had intentionally kept my distance, trying to heal and move on. Seeing his name on the screen stirred up a mix of emotions, but I knew I couldn't let the past hold me back.

As tempting as it was to reply, I made a conscious decision to focus on the present and the future I was building with Nico. I put my phone aside, choosing to immerse myself in my work and the positivity that surrounded me.

Throughout the day, my phone buzzed with sweet messages from Nico. *Just thinking about you*, one read. *Can't wait to see you later*, another said. His thoughtful gestures never failed to bring a smile to my face, reminding me of how lucky I was to have him in my life.

As our connection deepened, I started taking private salsa lessons with Nico at his dance school. With each lesson, I found myself growing more confident on the dance floor. It mirrored the newfound confidence I felt in our blossoming relationship.

One evening, as the sun began to set, we found ourselves at the gazebo in Buerkliplatz, overlooking the picturesque Zurich lake. The strains of salsa music echoed in the air as we swayed to the rhythm, our bodies moving in perfect harmony. People surrounding us were immersed in the salsa moves, creating an exhilarating atmosphere.

Nico pulled me close, his warm breath tickling my ear. "You're doing great," he whispered. "You're a natural."

I grinned, feeling a sense of pride in my progress. "I have an amazing teacher," I replied.

As the music played on, our steps becoming more synchronized with every beat, we took a moment to catch our breath. The serene atmosphere surrounding us felt almost magical.

Nico gently cupped my face in his hands, locking eyes with me. "I want you to know something," he said earnestly. "I'm falling in love with you, Erica."

My heart skipped a beat, and a rush of emotions washed over me. I felt my eyes welling up with tears of happiness and relief. "I'm falling in love with you too, Nico," I confessed, my voice barely above a whisper.

As the evening approached, I excitedly prepared myself for a night of dancing at Los Toros, the vibrant Latin club where Nico and I had planned to meet. He had informed me earlier that he had a family emergency and would join me a bit later with his brother, Sergio. I couldn't help but feel a mix of curiosity and concern for their family situation.

Natalia, always up for an adventure, joined me in getting ready. I couldn't help but share my apprehension about Sergio with her. "Just be careful, Natalia," I warned. "He can be quite the party animal."

She waved off my concerns with a mischievous smile. "Oh, I can handle him. Besides, who knows? Maybe he'll surprise us."

As the music pulsed through the club, Natalia and I took to the dance floor, swaying our hips to the infectious rhythm of reggaeton. The energy was electrifying, and despite Nico's absence, we were determined to make the most of the night.

After a few songs, Natalia and I retreated to the bar to catch our breath and sip on our drinks. We laughed and chatted, our excitement growing as we waited for Nico and his brother Sergio.

Finally, the moment arrived as the doors to Los Toros swung open, revealing the two Romeros. Nico looked dashing as ever, but there was a hint of stress in his eyes. Sergio, on the other hand, had a mischievous twinkle in his eye, ready for a night of fun.

"Hey, sorry for the delay," Nico said, flashing a warm smile despite the worry that still lingered. "Family stuff, you know."

"Of course," I replied, trying to hide my disappointment at the change in plans. "Is everything okay?"

"Yeah, it's just some business issues with one of our father's companies," Sergio chimed in, his voice nonchalant. "But we're here now, ready to dance and forget about it for a while!"

We joined them on the dance floor, and instantly, the stress seemed to fade away as we moved to the pulsating salsa beats. Nico and Sergio were remarkable dancers, leading Natalia and me with effortless grace.

As we twirled and spun under the colored lights, I couldn't help but notice the attention Nico and Sergio received from other club-goers. They were well known in Los Toros, and their charisma drew people to them like a magnet.

During a brief break, as we caught our breath on a nearby seating area, a statuesque Latina woman strode towards us with an air of confidence. Her dark, cascading curls framed a face adorned with sharp, expressive features. Her eyes blazed with intensity, accentuated by a sweep of smoky eyeshadow, and her lips were painted a bold shade of crimson. Clad in a form-fitting dress that accentuated her curves, she exuded a magnetic allure that commanded attention.

Natalia's expression shifted, and she leaned in close, her voice filled with concern as she whispered in my ear, "That's Nico's ex-girlfriend." The revelation sent a jolt of unease through me, unsure of the dynamics at play between Nico and this captivating woman. It caught me by surprise as this was not the woman I saw Nico having a good time with by the lake.

As the Latina woman drew closer, the tension in the air became palpable. Her piercing gaze locked onto Nico, her eyes filled with a mix of fury and hurt. The intensity of her stare seemed to penetrate his very soul, demanding answers and resolution.

At that moment, the club's vibrant energy seemed to dim. The pulsating beats fading into the background as the spotlight turned to this confrontation. Conversations hushed, heads turned, and all eyes were fixed on the unfolding drama.

With a voice filled with fury, she began shouting at him in rapid-fire Spanish. Although I didn't understand the words, the intensity of her voice sent chills down my spine. Nico stood his ground, his face a mask of conflicting emotions. His jaw clenched, revealing the inner turmoil he grappled with. I could sense the weight of their shared history hanging heavily in the air. The unspoken words and unresolved feelings fueling the tension between them.

Chapter 27

"Eva, please, let's talk somewhere private. This isn't the place for this," Sergio stepped forward, attempting to defuse the escalating confrontation.

But Eva's fury wouldn't be suppressed so easily. She squared her shoulders, her voice rising with every word.

"No, Sergio! I won't let him get away with this!" Her words reverberated through the club, drawing the attention of curious onlookers.

Nico's eyes bore into Eva's, a mix of regret and determination reflecting in their depths. He raised his hand in a calming gesture. "Eva, let's find a quiet corner and talk. We need to address this," he implored, his voice laced with sincerity and regret.

With a reluctant nod, Eva agreed, and the three of them walked outside the club, followed by Natalia and me, both feeling bewildered by the unfolding drama.

Outside, Eva's anger was still palpable. She shouted in Spanish, her emotions pouring out, her hand protectively on her stomach. Natalia and I watched the scene unfold, unable to comprehend the full extent of what was happening.

Nico, his expression a blend of exhaustion and desperation, turned to us with a pleading look. "Please, go back inside," he urged, his voice strained. "I'll explain everything later. Just trust me."

Reluctantly, we obeyed, casting worried glances over our shoulders. The music inside the club thumped relentlessly, a stark contrast to the turmoil we had left behind.

As we found a secluded corner, Natalia and I huddled together. I kept looking at the club's main door, hoping Nico would appear soon.

"What is all this about?" Natalia kept looking at me as if I had an answer.

I shrugged and continued staring at the door. It opened, but to my disappointment, instead of Nico, a woman appeared. I thought she would just pass by, but she walked straight towards us.

"Excuse me," she said, looking at me. "I couldn't help but overhear what happened. Are you two friends of Nico?"

"Yes, we are," Natalia shouted over the sound of music. "Do you know what's going on? We're completely in the dark."

"It seems Eva is claiming that Nico is the father of her unborn child. She's threatening to take him to court."

My heart sank at the revelation, the weight of the news crashing down on me. Natalia's eyes widened in shock as she processed the information.

"That... that can't be true, can it?" Natalia stammered. She looked at me, hoping I will deny it. "Nico mentioned nothing about a previous relationship or a child."

Tears welled up in my eyes, a mix of sadness, confusion, and betrayal flooding my emotions. I couldn't fathom how Nico had kept such a significant part of his life hidden from me.

My voice trembled. "How... how could he do this? I thought we had something special. I thought he was being honest with me!"

"We need to get out of here!" Natalia said firmly. "This is too much to handle. Let's find a taxi and go back to your place!" She grabbed my hand and made her way through the crowd. We walked outside, hailing a taxi that would take us away from the painful scene that had unfolded before us.

As we sat in the back of the cab, the weight of the situation settled heavily on my shoulders. Natalia reached out, grasping my hand in a gesture of comfort and solidarity.

"I can't even imagine what you're going through right now. But remember, you're not alone. We'll get through this together!"

I managed a weak smile, grateful for Natalia's unwavering support. As the cab driver wanted to drive away, someone banged on the door next to my seat.

"Erica!" Nico shouted. "Wait!"

I didn't want to look at him. "Drive, please," I urged the driver.

A baby on the way. Nico was going to be a father. There was nothing we could discuss right now. The tears continued to fall as we traveled back to my apartment; the streets passing by in a blur of lights and shadows.

Arriving home, the reality of the situation hit me like a tidal wave. The once-promising future I had envisioned with Nico now seemed shattered, scattered like broken fragments on the floor.

"We're going to get through this," Natalia said, determined. "Right now, you need rest and some time to process everything. Tomorrow, we'll figure out what steps to take next."

Nodding, I allowed Natalia to guide me into the apartment. Exhaustion weighed heavily on my shoulders, both physically and emotionally. I collapsed onto the couch, the events of the night replaying in my mind like a cruel loop.

The hours passed, a veil of darkness enveloping the city outside. As the first light of dawn crept through the windows, a soft knock echoed through the apartment.

"Who could that be at this hour?" Natalia asked.

Reluctantly, I made my way to the door, my heart heavy with anticipation. I opened it to find Nico standing there, his face pale and exhausted, his eyes filled with a mix of sorrow and determination. I wanted to slam the door in his face. The sight of him only intensified my pain and confusion. I wanted nothing more than to shut him out, to protect myself from further disappointment.

Nico held the door firmly. “Please, just hear me out! I need to explain,” he said. “I’m so sorry it took me the entire night to come here. I was at the hospital with Eva. She fell ill because of everything that happened, and I couldn’t leave her side.”

Natalia appeared next to me. “She doesn’t want to talk to you right now. You’ve hurt her enough!”

Nico was desperate. “I understand your anger, but I need her to know the truth. It’s not my baby, I swear it!”

Natalia didn’t give up. “But you were with her the entire night?”

“Yes,” Nico sighed. “I needed to make sure she received the care she needed. With my family’s reputation and all, I had to do it.”

The room fell silent as I struggled to process Nico’s words. Confusion and doubt warred within me, unsure of whom to believe. But deep down, a glimmer of hope flickered, yearning for the truth to shine through the darkness.

My voice was weak when I spoke. “Why should I believe you? How can I trust anything you say?”

"I know it's hard to believe me right now, but I'll do whatever it takes to prove it!" His eyes were pleading. "Eva's claims are false. I won't let them destroy what we have."

His words lingered in the air, but my heart remained heavy with doubt and sadness. The trust that had begun to blossom between us had been shattered, and the path forward seemed uncertain and treacherous. Tears streamed down my face once again as the weight of the situation bore down upon me. I looked at Natalia, seeking guidance, but she remained silent, allowing me to make my own decision.

"I can't deal with yet another heartache," I clenched my fists. "I knew there was something going on when she picked up your phone."

Nico's eyes widened. "You called me?"

I shook my head. "It doesn't matter anymore. Please delete my number."

I turned around and heard Natalia shutting the door behind me.

Chapter 28

The days following the incident with Nico and Eva were filled with a deep sense of pain and confusion. I found myself lost in a sea of emotions, questioning whether love was meant for me or if my heart was destined to be broken time and time again. Nico, despite my silence, continued to reach out, leaving voicemails and sending heartfelt texts, assuring me he would never give up on us.

"Erica, I understand that you're hurting," Natalia said. "But shutting yourself off from Nico completely might not be the answer. Maybe you should hear him out."

The thought of trying again scared me, yet I had this urge to be loved and needed. Being single might mean never having to worry about another person, but it also meant living a life of loneliness. The answer didn't seem clear; was I destined for a life of solitude or should I take the risk and put my heart on the line?

I sighed. "It's just so hard, Natalia. I don't know if I can trust him anymore. I don't even know if I can trust my own judgment."

"I get it," Natalia said. "But look at this beautiful bouquet of roses that arrived for you this morning. And there's a letter too."

I glanced at the stunning arrangement of flowers on my table and noticed the envelope tucked among them. With trembling hands, I opened the letter, my eyes scanning the heartfelt words Nico had written himself.

My dearest Erica,
I want you to know that I love you with all my heart.
The events with Eva have been incredibly painful
for both of us, but I want to assure you I am not
the father of her baby. It was a web of lies and deceit that I
had no control over. Please, give me a chance to prove my love
and devotion to you. I will do whatever it takes to make
things right and earn back your trust.
Yours forever,
Nico.

Tears welled up in my eyes as I read his words. I nev- er replied to his messages or letters, but I found solace in reading them, holding on to a glimmer of hope that maybe, just maybe, things could be different.

Natalia sat next to me on the sofa. "Erica, I know it's overwhelming," she said. "But you can't deny the connection you felt with Nico. It's not the same as it was with Tim. Nico is not giving up on you. Maybe it's time to give him a chance."

"I miss him, Natalia," I whispered. "I miss his presence, his laughter, his love. But can I really open my heart again after all this pain?"

"Only you can answer that question, darling. But remember, not all relationships are the same." Natalia looked at me, affection in her eyes. "Sometimes, we have to take a leap of faith to find the happiness we deserve."

Days turned into weeks, and the gifts and messages from Nico continued to arrive. He respected my physical space, but made it clear that he would never stop fighting for our love. The postman became a regular visitor, delivering packages that held the essence of Nico's love. There was a delicate necklace with a pendant in the shape of a heart, a symbol of his devotion. A handwritten poem arrived in the mail, inked with words that painted a vivid picture of our shared dreams and aspirations. A box filled with scented candles that reminded me of the day at Nico's apartment and the kiss we almost shared. I was eager to work from home more often, not just to take time for myself, but also to rush to the mailbox and rip open the envelopes containing letters from Nico. My hands trembled in anticipation as I waited for each new delivery. I found myself anticipating each little surprise, each token of his affection. It felt both terrifying and exhilarating. But I couldn't bring myself to face him. All the hurt I had been curating and putting away would resurface if I saw him in person.

One afternoon, there was a knock on my apartment door. Natalia, with her key for emergencies, entered with Sergio by her side. They both wore serious expressions, and my heart raced with anticipation.

Sergio cleared his throat. "Erica, I know this might seem surreal, but we have evidence that proves Eva's claims were false." He waved a piece of paper at me. "The DNA tests have confirmed that Nico is not the father of her baby. She was driven by greed and a desire for a piece of our family fortune!"

For weeks I had hoped to hear those words, but when they finally came, it was like a lightning bolt piercing through the air. My entire body went numb and all I could utter in disbelief was, "I...I don't know what to say. It's hard to believe".

"I understand," Sergio said. "But please, give Nico a chance to explain everything in person. We both know how much he loves you, and he's been through so much. Don't let Eva's deceit cloud your judgment."

Natalia joined in. "Sergio is right, Erica. This could be your chance at happiness. Don't let the pain of the past overshadow the possibility of a beautiful future."

As I listened to their words, a glimmer of hope began to spark within me. Maybe, just maybe, there was a chance for redemption and love. I took a deep breath and nodded, ready to take the leap of faith and meet Nico.

After all those weeks of beautiful letters and the love pouring out of them, I felt it was time. "Alright, I'll meet him."

A wide grin appeared on Sergio's face. "Nico will be overjoyed to hear that you're willing to give him another chance!"

Natalia smiled at me. "I knew you'd make the right decision, girl. Love has a funny way of finding its way back to us!" She looked at Sergio, smitten.

I was wondering what those two were up to while I isolated myself at home. I tried to process the whirlwind of emotions that had consumed my life in recent weeks. Excitement, trepidation, and a glimmer of hope danced within me. I couldn't deny the lingering doubts and fears, but there was a part of me that yearned for the possibility of a love that could conquer the darkest storms. Would I be able to forgive and forget? Could I trust Nico again? The doubts gnawed at me, but I reminded myself that love was built on resilience and the willingness to take risks.

"There is a salsa championship taking place at the Hallenstadion tonight," Sergio said, opening a website on his phone. "Nico had been practicing for hours. Why don't we surprise him?"

My heart fluttered with a mixture of nerves and excitement. The thought of surprising Nico at the salsa championship filled me with anticipation. I couldn't help but smile at the idea of seeing him on the dance floor, doing what he loved most.

Natalia's eyes sparkled with mischief as she joined Sergio in planning our surprise. "Yes, let's go and cheer him on! It will be the perfect way to show him you believe in him and the love you share."

Chapter 29

I stood in front of my closet, deliberating over which dress would capture the essence of the evening. I wanted something that would radiate joy and match the vibrant energy of the salsa championship. My eyes landed on a beautiful floral dress, its intricate patterns reminiscent of a blossoming garden.

As I glanced at myself in the mirror, I couldn't help but feel a surge of confidence. The dress embodied the essence of the evening, exuding both elegance and playfulness. It was a statement of my readiness to embrace the joy and celebration that awaited us.

With a final adjustment to my hair and a spritz of perfume, I felt ready to step into the night and into Nico's arms. The dress had become more than just an outfit—it was a symbol of my journey, a visual representation of the love and hope that had carried us through the storm.

I still couldn't believe that Eva had been lying all along. The weight that had burdened my heart for so long suddenly dissipated, replaced by a renewed sense of joy and relief. It was as if a heavy stone had been lifted off my chest, allowing me to breathe freely once again. At that moment, everything seemed to fall into place. The doubts and uncertainties that had plagued my mind now seemed insignificant in the face of the truth. It was a turning point, a chance for our love to blossom and grow stronger.

Natalia and I eagerly awaited Sergio's arrival, knowing that he would be our designated driver for the evening. Romero brothers refused to have a chauffeur, enjoying driving too much.

As his sleek, expensive car pulled up outside my apartment, we couldn't help but feel a sense of luxury and anticipation. We hopped into the backseat, exchanging excited glances as we embarked on our journey to the Hallenstadion in Zurich. As we arrived at the venue, the buzz of excitement permeated the air. The Romero family always had a VIP spot, and we were guided to seats close to the dancefloor. The energy was palpable, a mix of nerves and exhilaration as the crowd eagerly awaited the performances to come.

And then there he was. Nico took the stage, his presence commanding and magnetic. He danced with Isabella, his co-teacher, their movements fluid and captivating. The chemistry between them was undeniable, their performance leaving the audience in awe.

As I watched Nico dance, my heart swelled with a deep sense of pride and love. Every movement, every step showcased his unwavering dedication and talent. It was a beautiful sight to behold, his body moving in perfect harmony with the music, a true reflection of his artistry.

With each passing moment in the competition, my anticipation grew. The energy in the room was palpable as the couples showcased their unique styles and grace. But my eyes remained fixated on Nico, my heart racing with a mixture of nerves and excitement. I knew how much this competition meant to him.

And then the moment arrived. The announcement reverberated through the arena, declaring Nico and Isabella as the winners. The crowd erupted in thunderous applause, their cheers echoing throughout the space. The spotlight illuminated their triumphant figures. The journalists swarmed around them, capturing their victorious moment.

Amid the celebration, my gaze never wavered from Nico. I couldn't help but feel an overwhelming sense of joy and admiration for his incredible achievement. I longed to wrap my arms around him, to share in his triumph and tell him how proud I was.

The anticipation and excitement in my veins was electric as I waited outside the changing room, clutching a single red rose in my hand. When Nico emerged, his eyes widened with surprise and delight when he saw me. "Nico," I breathed out his name, filled with a rush of desire and love. I extended the rose towards him, my voice conveying all the emotion that was locked away in my heart. "This is for you, a symbol of everything I feel for you." He looked at the rose and then back at me, a wealth of unspoken feelings reflecting in his gaze. "Roses are usually for women," he murmured thoughtfully, "but I'll gladly accept it from you. It means more than words can express to me." My lips curved into a smile before they met his in an urgent kiss that seemed to last forever. In that moment, every doubt or uncertainty faded away as we connected on a level deeper than language could ever express. We had triumphed over our struggles together and nothing could break us apart.

Reunited with Nico, our hearts filled with newfound joy, we decided to celebrate our reunion by attending a lively salsa afterparty. Natalia and I joined Nico and Sergio on the dance floor, our bodies swaying to the infectious rhythms of the music.

As we danced together, the bond between us grew stronger with each step. My salsa moves might not have been perfect, but we were filled with enthusiasm and the joy of being together. Laughter echoed through the air as we twirled and spun, lost in the moment of pure happiness.

Being in Nico's arms again, surrounded by the love and support of Natalia and Sergio, I knew nothing could dampen our happiness. We had weathered the storm and come out stronger on the other side.

"I'm crazy about you. So—so—crazy," he kissed me between the words.

I chuckled. "So am I. You have no idea how often I thought about you."

Chapter 30

Nico's complete adoration and devotion to me nudged my heart away from its protective shell. He showered me with love and affection as we spent our free time wrapped up in each other's arms, rediscovering the things that had brought us together. I saw the way he looked at me, the way he whispered into my ear when no one else was listening. There were no games or tricks; he loved me for who I was, and I couldn't help but respond to his attentions.

Natalia and Sergio had made a special connection of their own, something that was both remarkable and a bit nerve-wracking to behold. Although Nico and I were somewhat hesitant about it, we chose to be encouraging instead. After all, love had an odd way of working out. We supported each other through the highs and lows of relationships; it was a beautiful relationship between us four, like a mutual understanding of the struggles and blissfulness of love.

As the weeks turned into months, our love grew deeper, and the future held promise and endless possibilities. We dreamed together, sharing our aspirations and desires for a life filled with love, adventure, and shared experiences.

One morning, as the sunlight poured through the windows, I discovered a small envelope slipped under my apartment door. Intrigued, I picked it up and saw my name written in Nico's elegant handwriting. Opening the envelope, I found a note that simply read, "Meet me tonight at 8 pm at the Dolder Grand Hotel. I have a surprise for you."

My heart raced with anticipation and curiosity. I couldn't help but wonder what Nico had in store for me. The Dolder Grand Hotel was renowned for its elegance and luxury. I couldn't help but be surprised that he had chosen such a prestigious venue for our evening together.

Natalia, sensing my excitement, came over to my apartment later that day. She wore a mischievous smile and behaved rather suspiciously. "Erica, my dear, we have some preparations to make for tonight," she said, her eyes twinkling with excitement. "I'll help you get ready, and I have a suggestion for an outfit that will match the grandeur of the Dolder."

Her suggestion was a stunning, floor-length gown that exuded elegance and sophistication. It was a departure from my usual style, but I trusted Natalia's impeccable taste. As I slipped into the dress, I felt a sense of transformation, as if I was stepping into a new chapter of my life.

As I admired myself in the mirror, Natalia beamed with delight. "Erica, you look absolutely breathtaking! This gown was made for you," she exclaimed, her eyes shining with pride.

I twirled around, feeling the fabric gracefully sway with each movement. "You have an impeccable eye for style, Natalia. I never would have chosen something like this, but it's perfect," I replied, grateful for her guidance.

Natalia chuckled, her mischievous smile returning. "Well, my dear, sometimes we need a little push out of our comfort zones to discover new facets of ourselves. Tonight is your night to shine."

The time came for me to leave, and as I stepped outside, I saw a sleek black car waiting for me. The hired family driver, dressed in a crisp uniform, greeted me with a warm smile. On the back seat was a single red rose, a symbol of love and romance. I took a seat, feeling a mix of excitement and nervousness, and allowed the driver to take me to the Dolder Hotel.

As the car glided through the city streets, my mind raced with questions and possibilities. What surprise awaited me at the Dolder? What had Nico planned? I couldn't help but feel a flutter of butterflies in my stomach, a mix of anticipation and joy.

Arriving at the Dolder Hotel, I stepped out of the car and marveled at the grandeur that surrounded me. The opulent building stood proudly, exuding an air of sophistication and luxury. I made my way inside, guided by the attentive hotel staff, and followed the path that led to the designated meeting place.

There, in a secluded corner of the hotel's elegant lobby, stood Nico, looking dashing. A smile spread across his face as he caught sight of me. "Erica, you look absolutely stunning," he said, his eyes filled with admiration and love.

I blushed, feeling a warmth spread through my cheeks. "Thank you, Nico. You've truly surprised me with this choice of location," I replied, my voice filled with a mixture of excitement and curiosity. "What is the surprise you have planned?"

Nico took my hand in his, leading me through the hotel's corridors. "You'll see," he said, his voice filled with a playful charm. "Just trust me and let the evening unfold."

We walked through the hotel's elegant corridors, the soft glow of chandeliers casting a romantic ambiance. With each step we took, I felt my heart beat faster, the anticipation building with each passing moment.

Finally, Nico led me to a private dining room, adorned with candlelit tables and breathtaking views of the city. It was a setting straight out of a fairy tale. The table was beautifully set, and the aroma of delicious cuisine filled the air.

As we took our seats, Nico's eyes never left mine. "Erica, I wanted to create a moment that we would cherish forever," he said, his voice filled with sincerity. "I want to show you how much you mean to me, and how grateful I am to have you in my life."

I felt my heart flutter with a mix of excitement and anticipation. The air in the room felt charged with emotion as Nico continued, his voice filled with love and vulnerability.

"Natalia once told me that love has a funny way of finding its way back to us," Nico said, his eyes locked on mine. "And in you, Erica, I've found a love that is pure, passionate, and all-consuming. You've brought light into my life, and I can't imagine my days without you."

Tears welled up in my eyes as I listened to his heartfelt words. Every doubt and fear that had plagued me seemed to melt away, replaced by a deep certainty that this love was worth fighting for.

Nico reached into his pocket, his hand trembling slightly. With a nervous smile, he pulled out a small velvet box and placed it gently on the table before me. My breath caught in my throat as he opened the box, revealing a dazzling diamond ring.

"Erica, will you make me the happiest man in the world? Will you marry me?" Nico asked, his voice filled with hope and anticipation.

I looked at him, the love in his eyes reflecting the love I felt in my heart. The room seemed to fade away, leaving only the two of us in a moment suspended in time.

Tears streamed down my face as I nodded, my voice choked with emotion. "Yes, Nico. Yes, a thousand times yes!"

Nico slipped the ring onto my finger, and in that instant, I felt an overwhelming sense of joy and contentment. We shared a passionate kiss, sealing our commitment to one another.

Natalia and Sergio approached our table, their faces beaming with happiness. They have been waiting outside the dining room all that time! Partners in crime to make sure me and Nico have our happy ending.

Natalia enveloped me in a tight hug. "Congratulations, my dear! I'm so happy for you both."

Sergio extended his hand to Nico, a proud smile on his face. "Well done, brother."

In the midst of the celebration, Nico pulled me aside, a mischievous smile playing on his lips. "There's one more surprise for you, my love," he whispered, his eyes sparkling with excitement. Curiosity ignited within me as he led me to a balcony overlooking the city's skyline. The cool breeze brushed against my skin, and the twinkling lights below added a touch of magic to the moment. Suddenly, the night sky erupted in a dazzling display of fireworks, illuminating the darkness with bursts of color and light. My breath caught in my throat as I watched the spectacle, my heart filled with wonder and awe. Nico turned to me, his eyes gleaming with love. "This is just the beginning, Erica," he said, his voice filled with promise. "I want to spend the rest of my life making you happy, creating moments like this filled with love, laughter, and endless adventure." Tears welled up in my eyes once again, but this time, they were tears of pure happiness. I took his hand in mine, my heart overflowing with gratitude for the love and happiness that surrounded us.

Chapter 31

The sun shone brightly in the clear sky, casting a warm glow over the lush garden where our wedding ceremony was about to take place. Since it was a Romero wedding, the appropriate venue had to be chosen. We went to the prestigious Baur Au Lac Hotel in Zurich. Its timeless elegance and impeccable reputation were well known. Stunning architecture, picturesque surroundings, and world-class service. All that made it the perfect choice to celebrate our special day in style and create unforgettable memories.

The walkway leading to the altar was adorned with delicate pink and white petals, creating a romantic and inviting path for the bride and groom. Towering trees surrounded the garden, their branches creating a natural canopy, casting dappled sunlight into the ceremony space. The air was filled with the sweet scent of blooming flowers.

It was a day filled with anticipation, excitement, and an abundance of love. As I stood before the mirror, my heart fluttered with a mix of nerves and joy. Natalia, my dearest friend and maid of honor, stood by my side, helping me with the final touches of my bridal attire.

My wedding dress was a vision of ethereal beauty. The intricate lace bodice hugged my curves, adorned with delicate beading that shimmered with every movement. The flowing skirt cascaded down in layers of tulle, creating a romantic and timeless silhouette. The back of the dress featured a stunning lace detail, adding a touch of allure to the elegant design.

"Erica, you look absolutely breathtaking! Nico is going to be speechless when he sees you." Natalia was beaming. My radiant maid of honor wore a pale pink dress that perfectly complemented the wedding's color palette.

I smiled, feeling a surge of happiness wash over me. The months leading up to this day had been a whirlwind of planning and preparation, but now everything felt just right. I was ready to take this step with Nico, ready to embark on a lifetime of love and companionship.

I took a deep breath. "Thank you, Natalia. I couldn't have asked for a better friend and maid of honor. Your support means the world to me."

"Oh, Erica, you know I'll always be here for you!" Natalia wiped a tear away. "This day is about celebrating the love you and Nico share, and I'm honored to be a part of it."

As I looked around the room, my heart swelled with gratitude at seeing my mother who had traveled all the way from the United States to celebrate my wedding with me. Her presence brought a sense of warmth and familiarity to the occasion. I approached her. Mom's eyes were glistening with emotion.

She took my hands in hers and said, "Erica, my dear, I never imagined this day would come. I was always worried that you would never find someone who truly understands and cherishes you. But look at you now, marrying the love of your life. It's a beautiful surprise, and I couldn't be happier for you."

Her words filled me with a profound sense of love and appreciation, and I embraced her tightly, whispering, "Thank you, Mom. This moment wouldn't be the same without you here."

With our emotions running high, we made our way to the garden, where family and friends had gathered, their eyes filled with anticipation. Sergio, Nico's brother and best man, waited to accompany me down the aisle.

"Ready for the grand entrance, Erica?" Sergio grinned. "This is a moment you'll cherish forever."

I smiled. "I am, Sergio. Thank you for being here for us, for your unwavering support."

Sergio placed his hand on my shoulder. "You and Nico are meant for each other. I've seen the love you two share, and it's a beautiful thing."

I blushed. Slightly trembling, I nodded to Sergio. I was ready. As the music swelled, I linked arms with Nico's brother, and together we walked down the aisle. All eyes were on us, but my gaze was fixed on Nico, who stood at the end, his eyes glistening with tears of joy.

"You look absolutely radiant, Erica," Nico whispered. "You've stolen my heart all over again."

The ceremony was filled with heartfelt vows, promises of love and devotion that echoed through the air. Our loved ones watched as we exchanged rings, sealing our commitment to one another.

Finally, the officiant ended the ceremony with a well-known sentence. A sentence that was a begging of a new adventure. "By the power vested in me, I now pronounce you husband and wife. You may kiss the bride."

As Nico leaned in to kiss me, the air was filled with applause and cheers. Our guests erupted in joyous celebration. Journalists swarmed the wedding venue, eagerly capturing every moment of the Romero wedding. Cameras flashed and reporters jotted down notes as they tried to get a glimpse of the newly married couple. The presence of the media added an extra layer of excitement and glamor to the already magical evening.

Later, when everyone took their places at the table, Natalia raised her glass. "To Erica and Nico, may your love shine bright, illuminating your path together! Cheers!"

Guests raised their glasses. "Cheers!"

As the evening progressed, the reception was filled with music, salsa dancing, and heartfelt speeches. The bond between our families grew stronger, and friendships were forged on this special day.

Natalia took the stage for the toast. "Ladies and gentlemen, if I can have your attention, please. Today, we celebrate not only the union of Erica and Nico, but also the power of love and friendship. I've had the privilege of witnessing their journey, and it fills my heart with joy to stand here as Erica's maid of honor. Erica, you have found a love that is steadfast and unwavering, and I have no doubt that you and Nico will create a lifetime of beautiful memories together."

Sergio joined Natalia on the stage. She handed him the microphone. "Nico, my brother, I've watched you grow into the man you are today, and I couldn't be prouder. Erica, you bring out the best in him, and I know that together, you will conquer any challenge that comes your way. May your love continue to flourish and may your journey be filled with laughter and happiness."

"To Erica and Nico!"

As I looked around the room, filled with the smiling faces of family and friends, I felt an overwhelming sense of gratitude and love.

I whispered to Nico. "This is the beginning of our forever, Nico. I love you with all my heart."

"And I love you," Nico squeezed my hand. "Today, we've promised to stand by each other's side, no matter what life throws our way. Our journey together starts now."

With those words, we danced under the starlit sky, surrounded by the love and support of those who had witnessed our love story unfold. It was a celebration of a love that had overcome obstacles and triumphed, a love that would continue to grow with each passing day.

As the night drew to a close, we bid farewell to our guests, our hearts filled with memories that would last a lifetime. Hand in hand, we walked into the beginning of our forever, knowing that love had brought us here and love would guide us through the years to come.

The Swiss newspapers were abuzz with articles about the elegant Romero wedding at the Baur Au Lac Hotel in Zurich. Headlines captured the romance and glamor of the event, showcasing the exquisite details of the ceremony and reception. The articles highlighted the breathtaking venue, the stunning wedding attire, and the joyous atmosphere shared by all. Our love story became a source of inspiration, symbolizing the power of love to overcome challenges and create a fairy-tale ending.

A few days after our wedding, I received a heartfelt note in the mail from Tim. He had come across an article about our wedding and took the opportunity to reach out and extend his congratulations. In his note, he expressed his genuine happiness for me and wished me all the best in my newfound happiness. It was a touching gesture that reminded me of the importance of closure and moving forward with love and goodwill.

Chapter 32

As we stepped off the plane and made our way through the bustling airport, the memories of our enchanting honeymoon in Colombia were still fresh in our minds. It had been a whirlwind adventure filled with breathtaking landscapes, vibrant cultures, and moments of pure bliss.

In Colombia, we explored the charming streets of Cartagena. We were wandering hand in hand through the colorful colonial architecture and soaking in the lively atmosphere. We immersed ourselves in the rhythms of salsa, dancing the night away with locals and embracing the passion and energy of the dance. We ventured into the lush coffee plantations of the Coffee Triangle, savoring the aroma of freshly brewed coffee and indulging in the rich flavors that awakened our senses.

But it wasn't just the picturesque landscapes or the vibrant cities that made our honeymoon special. It was the connection we shared, the way our love blossomed and deepened as we experienced new adventures together. From trekking through the dense jungles of Tayrona National Park to marveling at the majestic beauty of the Cocora Valley; each moment was an opportunity to strengthen our bond and create lasting memories.

Nico's love and devotion were unwavering, and he continued to shower me with affection and support. He was my rock, always there to lift me up when I needed it and to celebrate every joyous moment. Our conversations were filled with dreams and aspirations as we shared our hopes for the future and the life we envisioned together.

Natalia and Sergio were waiting eagerly at the arrival gate to greet us. Their smiles widened as they caught sight of us, their eyes brimming with excitement.

Natalia hugged me tightly, her voice filled with joy. "Welcome back, lovebirds! I hope you had the most amazing honeymoon."

We exchanged happy greetings, and soon we were on our way back to my small apartment. It had been a place of refuge and solace, but now it felt like a temporary stop on our journey together. We had plans to move into a new apartment, a space that would be just for us, where we could create a home filled with love and laughter.

Once we arrived at the apartment, Natalia and Sergio helped us with our luggage. Their excitement was palpable. They chatted animatedly about their own plans and how happy they were for us. As Natalia and Sergio made their way to the door, I took a deep breath, feeling a mix of nervousness and excitement. "Wait, before you go, I have a surprise for Nico."

Curiosity flickered in Nico's eyes as I handed him a small box adorned with a bow. He looked at me questioningly, his hands trembling slightly as he opened it. Inside were a pair of tiny baby socks, their soft fabric a symbol of the new chapter that awaited us.

Nico's eyes widened, and his breath caught in his throat. He looked at me, his voice barely a whisper. "Are you saying...?"

I nodded, a radiant smile spreading across my face. "Yes, Nico. We're going to have a baby."

Emotion washed over Nico, his eyes welling up with tears of joy and disbelief. He pulled me into a tight embrace, his voice filled with overwhelming happiness. "I can't believe it. I'm going to be a father. This is the most incredible surprise, Erica."

Natalia's eyes widened with excitement as she looked at me. "Oh my goodness, Erica! This is incredible news! We're going to be aunt and uncle!"

Sergio grinned from ear to ear, his voice filled with joy. "Congratulations, Nico! You're going to be an amazing father. I can't wait to spoil this little one rotten."

Tears of happiness streamed down my face as we held each other, our hearts overflowing with love and anticipation of the new life growing within me. We reveled in the joy of the moment, knowing that our love had created something truly beautiful.

In that small apartment, amidst the packed boxes and the promise of a new beginning, our love story took another extraordinary turn. Our journey as husband and wife had now expanded to include the miraculous journey of parenthood. We knew that our love would continue to grow, creating a future filled with endless possibilities and cherished memories.

Epilogue

As I sat in my elegant dress, surrounded by the grandeur of the Romero's wedding, I couldn't help but feel a pang of envy as I watched the newlyweds bask in their happiness. It seemed like they had found the kind of love and joy that had eluded me for far too long.

My husband Markus sat beside me, his attention focused on his phone. It was as if he had forgotten I was even there. We were still in our thirties, but the spark that once ignited our relationship had faded over the years. The demands of his banking career had consumed him, leaving little room for the affection and love that used to define our marriage.

I longed for the days when we would laugh together, hold hands, and share intimate moments. But now, it seemed like we were two strangers living under the same roof, leading separate lives. The once passionate and romantic man I fell in love with had become an ambitious banker, always chasing success and recognition.

As I discreetly glanced at Markus, his eyes glued to the screen, I couldn't help but feel a wave of loneliness wash over me. I yearned for his attention, his affection, and the reassurance that I was still the woman he desired. But it seemed like the only passion he had left was for his work, his pursuit of climbing the corporate ladder in one of Switzerland's largest banks.

I had tried to express my feelings to him, but my words seemed to fall on deaf ears. He would listen briefly, nod his head, and promise to make more time for us. But those promises were never fulfilled, overshadowed by his relentless dedication to his career.

As I watched the newlyweds exchange vows and dance their first dance, a mix of emotions swirled within me. I couldn't help but wonder if I would ever experience that kind of deep connection and happiness again. Was this the fate of every woman who married a successful banker? To be left longing for love and affection, overshadowed by the demands of their profession?

I took a deep breath, attempting to push away the melancholy that threatened to consume me. I deserved more than this, more than a loveless marriage that had become nothing more than a transaction of convenience.

At that moment, I made a silent vow to myself. I would no longer settle for a love that was absent. I would reclaim my happiness, whether it meant rekindling the flame in our relationship or finding it elsewhere.

With newfound determination, I turned to Markus. His eyes were still fixed on his phone, oblivious to the turmoil within me. I placed my hand gently on his arm, hoping to capture even a sliver of his attention.

"Markus," I said, my voice tinged with a mixture of sadness and determination. "We need to talk. It's time we address the state of our marriage and the lack of love and connection between us. I refuse to settle for anything less than the happiness we both deserve."

He looked up from his phone, surprise flickering in his eyes. In that moment, I hoped to see a glimmer of the man I once knew, the man who made me feel alive. Whether he could meet me halfway and breathe life back into our relationship remained to be seen. But one thing was clear: I would no longer allow myself to be overshadowed by the pursuit of success in his banking career.

I, Jessica Brunner, will no longer just be a banker's wife.

Coming soon

Part 2 of **Elsewhere Love** Series

Afterword

As I sit down to write this afterword, reflecting on the journey that led me to this moment, I am filled with an overwhelming sense of gratitude. For the past 15 years, Switzerland has been my home, and Zurich, with all its ups and downs, has become an integral part of my life. It is a city that has embraced me, nurtured my growth, and inspired me in countless ways.

But Zurich is not just a backdrop; it is a character in its own right, a silent protagonist that weaves through the narrative, leaving an indelible mark on the story. Its streets became the stage for the protagonists' journeys, the scenes unfolding against the backdrop of iconic landmarks like the Bahnhofstrasse and the Bellevue. Through their eyes, the readers could experience the pulse of the city, its energy, and its unique spirit.

Yet, as much as Zurich shaped the story, there was another passion of mine that demanded a place within its pages. My newfound love for Latin dance had to find its way into the tale. The vibrant rhythms, the fiery movements, and the sheer joy that dance brought into my life had to intertwine with the tapestry of Zurich's beauty.

Thank you for joining me on this literary journey, and may you find your own passion within these pages.

With heartfelt gratitude,
Klaudia

About the Author

·♥·♥·♥·♥·♥·

With a passion for storytelling, Klaudia enjoys crafting engaging narratives for both children and adults. Her debut romance book, "How to be in relationship," showcases her romantic spirit and invites readers into a world of love, growth, and connection. As she explores the complexities of human relationships, her heartfelt stories inspire, uplift, and entertain. Keep an eye out for Klaudia Sonas' upcoming projects as she continues to share her storytelling with her readers.

Newsletter (updates, giveaways and freebies)

For bonus goodies delivered straight to your inbox, sign up for the newsletter to stay in the loop.

www.klaudiasonas.com

Keep in touch!

Don't miss a beat in Klaudia's writing journey! Make sure to follow her on social media for all the latest news, updates, and exciting giveaways.

https://www.instagram.com/klaudiasonas

ARC Readers

Would you like to sign up to become an Advanced Copy Reader?

Sign up here **www.klaudiasonas.com**

www.ingramcontent.com/pod-product-compliance
Lightning Source LLC
LaVergne TN
LVHW091408190726
843491LV00006B/1325

* 9 7 8 3 9 5 2 5 8 3 2 6 5 *